By the bestselling authors of
Specky Magee
Specky Magee and the Great Footy Contest
Specky Magee and the Season of Champions
Specky Magee and the Boots of Glory
Specky Magee and the Legend in the Making
and
Specky Magee and the Spirit of the Game

PUFFIN BOOKS

Published by the Penguin Group
Penguin Group (Australia)
250 Camberwell Road, Camberwell, Victoria 3124, Australia
(a division of Pearson Australia Group Pty Ltd)
Penguin Group (USA) Inc.
375 Hudson Street, New York, New York 10014, USA
Penguin Group (Canada)
90 Eglinton Avenue East, Suite 700, Toronto, Canada ON M4P 2Y3
(a division of Pearson Penguin Canada Inc.)
Penguin Books Ltd
80 Strand, London WC2R 0RL England
Penguin Ireland
25 St Stephen's Green, Dublin 2, Ireland
(a division of Penguin Books Ltd)
Penguin Books India Pvt Ltd
11 Community Centre, Panchsheel Park, New Delhi – 110 017, India
Penguin Group (NZ)
67 Apollo Drive, Rosedale, North Shore 0632, New Zealand
(a division of Pearson New Zealand Ltd)
Penguin Books (South Africa) (Pty) Ltd
24 Sturdee Avenue, Rosebank, Johannesburg 2196, South Africa

Penguin Books Ltd, Registered Offices: 80 Strand, London, WC2R 0RL, England

First published by Penguin Group (Australia), 2009

10 9 8 7 6 5 4 3 2 1

Cover design by John Canty and Brad Maxwell © Penguin Group (Australia)
Author and cover photographs by John Tsiavis, additional photography by John Canty
Statue of Leigh Matthews by Louis Laumen
Typeset in 12/18 New Baskerville by Post Pre-press Group, Brisbane, Queensland
Printed and bound in Australia by McPherson's Printing Group, Maryborough, Victoria
Colour separation by Splitting Image

National Library of Australia
Cataloguing-in-Publication data:

Arena, Felice.

Specky Magee and the battle of the young guns / Felice Arena, Garry Lyon.

ISBN: 978 0 143 30466 1 (pbk.)

A823.3

puffin.com.au

Specky Magee
& the battle of the young guns

Felice Arena &
Garry Lyon

Puffin Books

G'day all!

Specky is back! Woo-hoo! It's been a long couple of footy seasons since the last book, so we've packed this latest with the best of everything you'd expect from a Specky Magee novel. Only there's more! More footy action, more drama, more romance (ew!), more comedy (Danny and Robbo are up to their old tricks) and even more mystery (who is that dude following Specky?).

But whilst we've had a fun time creating and writing these stories, there's an entire team busily working hard behind the scenes to make sure these books make it to you. Like Specky, we value teamwork. It inspires us to 'put in the hard yards' and be the best we can be. We want to shout out a massive thanks to Michelle Madden, Laura Harris, Kristin Gill, Sally Bateman, Julia Ferracane, John Canty and all the other talented folk at Penguin. This is a team we're very proud to be part of.

So, welcome back, loyal Specky fans. And welcome to new readers if this is your first book. We hope you enjoy this story as much as we enjoyed writing it.

As you can tell we're a little excited about this one and we're finding it hard to 'keep a lid on it'. So kick off your boots, get comfortable and enjoy *Specky Magee and the Battle of the Young Guns*.

Felice and Garry

P.S. For all the latest news about all things Specky, remember to check in at www.speckymagee.com or www.felicearena.com

1. a closer look

The plane touched down and taxied towards the terminal.

'Welcome to Adelaide . . .' The captain's voice echoed through the speakers. 'The temperature this afternoon is a very pleasant twenty degrees Celsius. The local time is one-forty p.m. Once again, we welcome the international travellers who joined us in Victoria and apologise for the delay we experienced at Melbourne Airport. Thank you for flying with us and we hope you enjoy your stay in South Australia.'

As the plane jolted to a halt, there was a wave of frenzied motion: passengers unbuckled their belts, jumped to their feet, and reached for their bags in the overhead lockers. At the front of the plane, in business class, a bald man in a suit moved to the door to make sure he was first to exit.

Almost jogging, he hurried to the baggage carousels. While he was impatiently waiting for his luggage to appear, his mobile rang.

'Hello,' he said. 'Yes! Just got here . . . I don't know, but I hope so. It'll be good to finally get a look at him. No, I'm gonna check into my hotel first – drop off my bag. Which, by the way, has just appeared on the belt . . . Okay, yep, talk to you later.'

He grabbed his bags, jogged to the hire-car counter and picked up his keys. Then he drove out of the airport parking lot as if he were in the final lap of a grand prix.

Bursting into his hotel room, the man tossed his bag on the bed and switched on the TV. His mobile rang again.

'Hello. Yes, I'm here. Look, I can't talk now – they're telecasting the game . . . When I checked in, I asked for directions to the ground and the porter said it's being aired live on Cable.' As he spoke, the bald man frantically clicked through the channels. 'Here it is! Found it! I don't believe it – I think that's him on screen right now! I'm telling you, this kid is the real deal – I know there are no guarantees in this caper, but this lad might be the best prospect I've ever laid eyes on. Yeah . . . Trust me on this one. Talk later.'

The man dropped his phone and turned up the volume to hear the commentary . . .

2. courage

. . . and here he is again – young Simon Magee for the Vics – about to have his fifth shot at goal. He hasn't quite had his kicking boot on today, managing two goals and two behinds, but the boy has lived up to all the hype surrounding him over the past week.

I agree, Jim. This kid has been one of the stars of this Under-Fifteen national football carnival. He didn't have this problem two days ago when the Big V smashed the boys from Tasmania. His six-goal display was the standout performance of the week, and right now he's the equal leading goal-kicker of the entire carnival. And we're in for a bit of a shoot-out because right now, at the other end of the ground, the big lad from Western Australia, Mitch Mahoney, has four goals for the game and has drawn level with young Magee.

You're dead right, Brian. Magee starts his run-up . . . He's only thirty metres out, on a slight angle, and if he kicks this one he'll take the outright lead again. He makes good contact – it looks good . . . but no! It just drifts off line, and he has to settle for a behind. And there goes the siren, with the Vics leading Western Australia by just seven points, with the winner to take on South Australia in the National Final in three weeks' time. And remember that the Final is a curtain-raiser to the biggest game of the AFL season, and one of the biggest sporting events in the country, the AFL Grand Final. What an opportunity for these young boys!

Specky kicked at the ground, disappointed that he had missed such an easy shot.

'Don't worry, Speck. Get the next one.'

His good mate, Brian Edwards, was the first of his team-mates to offer his encouragement.

As the two jogged towards the three-quarter-time huddle, the rest of the team joined Brian in supporting Specky, and urged each other on.

'Come on, boys. One last quarter and we'll be playing on the G on Grand Final Day.'

'Thirty more minutes and we get the chance to be National Champions.'

'Suck it in, fellas! Biggest quarter of our lives coming up.'

Playing for Victoria was everything Specky had hoped it would be. The most talented Under-Fifteen footballers from around the State had come together to play under the legendary junior football coach Jay 'Grub' Gordan. Specky couldn't believe how lucky he was to be playing at this level. He was used to being the best in his team, but here he was test-ing himself against elite young footballers from around the country and playing alongside the best of the best.

'Righto, settle down. Get a drink and listen up,' ordered Grub.

The chatter stopped immediately. All eyes focused on the short, grey-haired coach with the gravelly voice who had, in the space of a couple of weeks, united this group into a tight-knit team, prepared to do whatever he asked of them.

'Geez, Simon,' he said, frowning. 'How did you miss that? Don't lean so far back when you make contact.'

Specky and his team-mates had learnt early on that they needed a thick skin to play under Grub. He was direct – pulled no punches – but was always constructive with his criticism.

'We're not gonna let these sandgropers take away our spot on the MCG!' another voice boomed. 'Come on, dig deep! Find something! Don't let the Big V down!'

Specky smiled. It was Dicky Atkins, a tough kid from Gippsland. He was a mountain of a boy, who already had hair on his massive chest. Sometimes Specky wondered if Dicky wasn't really an eighteen-year-old posing as a fourteen-year-old. No one took playing for Victoria more seriously than Dicky. He was the spirit of their side, constantly encouraging and supporting his mates. He never shut up on the ground, barking instructions and always giving 110%. He was, by far, the most popular member of the side, and his attitude set the tone for the rest of the team – especially when he was roaring encouragement at the top of his lungs.

'Okay, this is what we're going to do,' announced Grub. 'We're kicking into a slight breeze and we know that they'll kick the ball to Mahoney every time they go inside fifty. Dicky has done a fantastic job keeping Mahoney to just four goals, but we're going to give him a little support.'

Grub turned to Specky.

'Magee, I want you to play at half-back. We watched tapes through the week of Luke Hodge and the role he plays at Hawthorn. Well, I want you to do a similar job here.'

Specky was very familiar with the role that Luke Hodge had played in Hawthorn's Premiership victory. Luke's coach, Alastair Clarkson, had moved him from the centre of the ground, where he was one of the best mid-fielders in the competition, to the half-back line. It made it much more difficult for opposition clubs to tag him. In the process, Hodge was able to patrol the back line, reading the play expertly and, at the right time, leave his opponent and 'zone off' to help out his fellow defenders. Because he was such a beautiful kick, he was able to set up many of Hawthorn's attacking moves from the back line.

Opposition clubs really struggled to stop his influence, so much so that he went on to win the Norm Smith Medal as the best player on the ground. Specky knew that half-back had become one of the most important positions on the ground and he was excited about the challenge Grub had given him.

'You've still got responsibility for your opponent,' added Grub. 'But wherever possible I want you to get back in front of Mahoney and help out as much as you can.'

Grub finished his address and the team broke up and headed to their positions for the final quarter knowing that their shot at the National title at the MCG was at stake.

★ ★ ★

There's no doubt about Grub Gordan, Jimbo. He's swung another surprise. It looks as if young Magee is lining up at half-back. Why would he do that when Magee leads the goal kicking for the carnival and the Vics are only seven points up?

The commentators, Brian Paylor and Jim Bradshaw, were treating this game as seriously as any AFL match.

He's always done it, Brian. He doesn't want these boys becoming one-position players early in their careers. He likes to play them at both ends.

Specky found himself matched up on a much smaller half-forward flanker, Dylan Haddon.

The Western Australian runner came sprinting out to the nippy little player.

'Coach wants you to play out wide, drag Magee out of the play,' he said, in earshot of Specky. 'He doesn't care if you don't get a kick, just make sure *he* doesn't.'

Specky's opponent nodded, and immediately ran towards the boundary line, but Specky – remembering what Grub had said about the role of the 'sweeper' – only followed him halfway to the boundary. He turned and saw Dicky standing shoulder to shoulder with Mitch Mahoney – the great Western Australian hope – bumping into him and chattering into his ear. They were the only two players inside the Vics' defensive fifty.

Right, thought Specky. I've got to stay close enough to Dicky that I can get back and cut off any passes to Mahoney, but I've also got to keep a close eye on Haddon.

The Vics have dominated the first seven minutes of the quarter, Brian. I don't think the sandgropers have gone inside fifty yet.

Specky was enjoying his view of the game from the half-back flank. He hadn't been called upon to do anything yet and that was fine by him. The mid-field were in control, led by Brian and the Vics' rover, 'Bear' Gleeson, but they hadn't made it pay on the scoreboard. They still led by only nine points.

The ball's kicked in from full-back and is marked strongly by Western Australia – beautiful quick hands! And they're out in space, bouncing down the wing. This is the big chance for the boys from the West. Where is Mahoney? They'll be looking for him!

Specky quickly looked to Haddon, his blond opponent. He was standing close to the boundary, not really interested in calling for the ball. Specky made a split-second decision. He left him and headed towards Dicky and Mitch Mahoney.

Mahoney goes one way and then the other, and now he makes his lead. Oh no! Atkins has stumbled. Mahoney's in the clear and that's where the ball is going.

Specky saw Dicky trip and ran harder, back with the flight of the ball. He could see that Dicky was not going to get there to make the spoil – it was all down to him now.

It's a beautiful pass and Mahoney's in the clear. Look out! Who's that?

At full stretch, with eyes on the ball, Specky dived – all the time aware that big Mitch Mahoney was hurtling towards him. His fist made contact with the ball centimetres before Mahoney arrived at full steam with his arms outstretched. Specky heard the crowd go crazy a second before they collided with a sickening thud.

. . . and Magee gets there, punching the ball clear towards the boundary line! What an effort, Jimmy! That takes some pretty exceptional courage, right there.

It does, Brian, from both players. Let's not forget that young Mahoney never put in a short step and didn't take his eyes off the ball either.

Good point, Jim. That's what you get in this National Carnival – the best kids playing the very best footy. I love it.

3. dicky

'That was a great result, boys,' beamed Grub. 'Really well done! Now we look forward to three weeks' time when we take on the South Australians at the MCG. By the time the last quarter comes around there could be close to one hundred thousand people there. It will be an experience you'll never forget.'

Specky smiled despite his aching body and the bruises that were starting to turn blue where he had smashed into Mitch Mahoney at full speed. It had been worth it to get into the final.

Grub finished his post-game talk, and Bobby Stockdale – Grub's long-time assistant coach – gave the team their itinerary for the next three weeks. They would fly home that afternoon and

14

would train twice a week in the lead-up to the final. They were all encouraged to look after themselves – ice up any sore spots, rehydrate with plenty of Gatorade and water, and do a good cool-down.

Just as the boys were about to head to the showers, Dicky Atkins stood up on one of the rundown benches. Specky was used to Dicky's big after-the-game speeches, which were usually just a string of lame jokes, many at his own expense, and were often delivered wearing only a jockstrap. Everyone started laughing and yelling at him, and he was bombarded with rolled-up bits of discarded ankle tape and well-sucked orange peels. Usually, Dicky loved the attention, but this time he wasn't laughing along.

'Nah, come on! Shut up, everyone!' he bellowed. 'I want to be serious for a minute.'

'Well, put some pants on – that might help!' yelled Lenny Morgan, the team's cheeky number-one rover from the Melbourne suburb of Broadmeadows. He shaved his head before every game as part of his pre-game ritual, so everyone called him 'Skull'.

Specky and the others burst into laughter and even Dicky smiled.

'Look, I just wanted to say how much today meant to me,' he said. 'We didn't know each other six weeks ago, and now I look at each and every one of ya, and I think – what a great bunch of mates! It feels like I've got a truckload of new brothers.'

Dicky's comment made Specky think of his best friends at school, Danny Castellino and Josh 'Robbo' Roberts. He wished they were there to see him play, but like Dicky, he now thought of some of his State team-mates as his closest friends as well. Specky looked around the room. The jokes had stopped. Even though Dicky looked like a hairy jungle beast at a circus, he had everyone's attention.

'I've realised that you'll only ever be as good as the dude sitting next to ya, and I don't mind say-ing that today, out there, I was struggling a bit.' Dicky's voice was a bit croaky and he had to clear his throat before he could go on. 'That kid I was playing on was bloody good, and there were a couple of times where he had me.'

The room was now deadly quiet.

'The game was in the balance and if they had scored another goal we might've been in trouble. When Mahoney led for that ball and I tripped over, I thought we were stuffed. And then one of my brothers made a decision.'

Specky squirmed in his seat as Dicky turned to him. All eyes were now on him.

'You put everything on the line for me, Speck,' exclaimed Dicky. 'For me and the rest of the guys. That Mahoney bloke could have taken you out. It was one of the gutsiest things I've ever seen.'

Specky couldn't believe it. He knew Dicky loved his footy, but he never dreamed he could get so emotional about it.

'I won't forget that, Speck. I won't let you down at the MCG, mate. I'm gonna do whatever it takes.'

With that, Dicky jumped off the bench and sat down. No one knew what to say.

'Someone get a tissue for the big fella! And don't forget the violins!' roared Skull, as he made his way over to Dicky and slapped him on the back. Dicky laughed as the rest of the room broke out in whoops and whistles. The ice had been broken.

As the rest of the boys finished showering and prepared to board the bus, Specky made his way over to Dicky. Seeing how emotional Dicky had been made him realise how important this competition was to all of them. It was life or death. Getting into the final had been the biggest thing in their lives, and Specky hadn't dared to think that they might actually get there. He was starting to understand what Grub meant when he said that the final would be a 'sliding doors' moment. This single match could determine what direction their lives went in – whether or not they had a future in football. If they were serious about making it to an elite level, it would be in this match where they would be expected to put their absolute best on show.

'Thanks, mate, that means a lot to me. I don't know how you can get up and speak like that, but it's pretty cool.'

'No worries, Speck. I meant every word,' replied Dicky, springing to his feet and giving Specky a big sweaty hug. 'It's just me, mate. I've always been like that. Me mum says I've always been kind of emotional. She's always told me never to be scared to show how ya feel, so that's what I do. And I don't give a crud what others think.'

★ ★ ★

The boys arrived at Adelaide airport an hour later and made their way to the departure gate. They were all dressed in navy team blazers with the Big V proudly displayed on their breast pockets. Total strangers at the airport asked Specky and his team-mates about the result of the game and offered their congratulations. For a moment, Specky could imagine what it was like for his AFL heroes as they wandered through airports around the country.

 The Victorian players had been lectured on the need to represent their State in the most positive light when they were out in public. They were easily identifiable as Victorian players, because of their uniform, and they were constantly reminded of the need to conduct themselves in a manner that reflected positively on their State and their families. Specky was aware that at AFL level, major sponsors – who poured in big money to be associated with various clubs – had been known to withdraw their funding due to unacceptable behavior from members of the team they were aligned with.

But not everyone wished them well. There was plenty of good-natured ribbing from the locals about how the South Australians were going to take the title in three weeks' time.

As Specky and Brian ordered themselves a smoothie from a juice shop, a bald-headed man who had just been served turned to them and smiled.

'Well played, boys,' he said. 'Especially you, young Magee. I liked what I saw!'

'Gee, there are some passionate footy supporters here,' said Brian, as Specky watched the stranger disappear into the queue boarding a flight to Melbourne. 'You're a rock star now, Speck. They even know your name.'

Specky laughed it off as they took a seat at their boarding gate. His body was still aching from the big last-quarter collision, but he couldn't remember a time when he'd felt happier or more excited about the weeks ahead.

4. response

Specky was relieved when the plane touched down in Melbourne. He had been away for over a week and, although he would never admit it to anyone, he was really looking forward to getting back home. He especially missed his new baby brother, Jack, who he was obsessed with – except when he woke the house screaming at three in the morning.

Specky and his State team-mates made their way to the baggage carousel where their excited families were waiting. As Specky scanned the crowd for his dad, he caught sight of the bald man who had congratulated him back at Adelaide airport. Specky stood still, not knowing whether he should acknowledge him or not.

Thwomp! came a punch to his arm.

'How'd you go, hotshot?'

Specky was surprised to find Alice, his big sister, standing there, and while he would never tell her in a million years, he was happy to see her.

'What are you doing here?'

'Nice way to greet your big sister who cancelled all her plans to come to the airport and greet the homecoming hero, the golden child of our household.'

'Yeah, right,' Specky laughed, yanking his suitcase off the carousel. 'You wouldn't be here unless you had no choice. Where's Dad?'

'He's in the car waiting for you. And you're right. He picked me up from Dieter's house on the way out here. Dieter wanted some space. He's full-on studying for exams at the moment.'

Dieter McCarthy – who Specky and his friends called the Great McCarthy – was Alice's boyfriend. He was a year older than she was, and was studying for his VCE.

'Sounds to me as if he might be finally coming to his senses,' Specky stirred. 'I think the Great McCarthy is about to give ya the flick, Al.'

'Shut up, boy wonder! What would you know

22

anyway? Just 'cause Christina has moved on and left you with a broken heart doesn't mean that true love doesn't exist elsewhere.'

Specky ignored her and rolled his luggage towards the exit signs, farewelling his team-mates as he left. The mention of his former girlfriend, Christina, was a bit of a low blow as it was still a sensitive subject, although they had both decided it was time to move on. Living in different cities had been too tough.

'Hey, Dad!' Specky beamed as he and Alice approached his father who was waiting by the car.

'Welcome back, kid,' he said, hugging Specky before loading the cases into the boot. 'Better hop in before we get a ticket.'

The Magees pulled out into the traffic and hit the freeway for the journey home. Specky sat in the front and an uneasy silence came over the car.

'Um, is anyone going to ask me about the carnival? We did finish equal top, you know. How awesome is it that we'll get to play at the MCG on Grand Final Day?!'

'Yes, of course – sorry, son,' said his dad.

'Robbo and Danny have been ringing non-stop, wondering what time you'll be home. They saw you on TV. We all did. On that sports channel.'

Specky smiled at the thought of his best friends' enthusiastic reaction. He had expected that. But his dad didn't seem as interested as he usually was. Mr Magee was the owner of a successful art gallery and would never have tuned into the sports channel if it wasn't for Specky's passionate love of football, but he was normally excited about Specky's success and was very supportive. Over the past couple of years he had come to appreciate what it meant to his son and had taken a much greater interest. So Specky was a bit surprised by his dad's low-key response.

'Yeah, that was pretty incredible. It was the most unbelievable week,' added Specky. 'Grub is an awesome coach and we played at AAMI Stadium and the Adelaide Oval. I still can't believe that we knocked off Western Australia, Tasmania and Queensland. It'll be a massive game against South Australia at the G.'

'You've certainly got a lot to look forward to,' said Mr Magee, sounding distracted. He pulled into a service station. 'Won't be a minute, guys,' he said, hopping out of the car.

'What's eating him?' Specky asked Alice, who was sitting in the back staring aimlessly out the window.

'He's been grumpy for a couple of days now,' she said. 'Ever since Grandpa Ken arrived from Perth.'

Specky twisted around to face her.

'Grandpa Ken? You mean Dad's dad? He's here?' he said. 'In Melbourne?'

'No, genius, he joins us every night via satellite – of course he's here in Melbourne.'

'Well, why didn't anyone tell me?' protested Specky. 'I mean, it's been, like, ten years since we've seen him. Why's he here all of a sudden?'

'I dunno really – I assumed he wanted to meet Jack.' Alice shrugged. 'It was a bit unexpected. He just showed up at the door and asked if he could stay for a couple of weeks. Just like that. Well, you know what Mum's like – she couldn't say no, even though she clearly wanted to. She's exhausted with Jack. The last thing she needs is a guest out of the blue.'

'Woah, how did Dad cop that?' asked Specky.

He knew his father had a strained relationship with Grandpa Ken.

'How would I know? I'm not Dr Phil,' said Alice. 'I've got my own problems to worry about. Like why my so-called boyfriend can't seem to find the time to hang out with me. All I know is that Dad has been like a bear with a sore head since Grandpa arrived.'

5. grandpa ken

'Welcome back, darling,' said Specky's mum as the three of them spilled in through the front door of their Camberwell home. She gave Specky a huge suffocating hug. 'I've missed you so much. What a great job you did. We're so proud of you. We saw every minute of the game on TV. But you almost gave me a heart attack when you got knocked over in the last quarter.'

At least someone is happy to see me, thought Specky as he struggled to free himself from his mum's hug.

'Thanks, Mum,' he said. 'Whipped up anything special for me?'

'Are you kidding?' snapped Alice. 'The chosen one has returned! We must honour him with plentiful gifts of the finest food.'

'Now, Alice, don't be silly,' said Mrs Magee. 'You know I don't play favourites in this house.'

'Yeah, right! She's been cooking all day for you, boofhead,' Alice said. 'Your favourite vegetable soup is on the stove and there's a massive vegetarian lasagna in the oven that would feed a small African village.'

'That's good, 'cause I'm mighty hungry,' came a booming voice from the lounge room. 'Now, where's this champion grandson of mine? Give us a look at the next Nick Riewoldt!'

Grandpa Ken entered the kitchen. He was just as Specky remembered him – with very blue eyes and a grin defined by his thick grey moustache. Specky thought he looked a little like Melbourne legend Ron Barassi.

'Simon, do you remember Grandpa Ken?' asked Specky's mum. 'It's been quite a while since you've seen him.'

'I'll go and check on Jack,' muttered Mr Magee. Specky caught his dad rolling his eyes as he left the room.

Specky raised his arm to shake his grandpa's hand.

'What's this nonsense, son? I'm your grandpa. Come here and give us a hug!' Specky awkwardly moved forward to greet Grandpa Ken with a hug.

'Come with me, lad,' added Grandpa Ken, gesturing for Specky to join him in the lounge room.

Specky really wanted to unpack and call his mates. But a raised eyebrow from his mother suggested that wasn't an option. He pulled a face at her as he followed his grandpa out of the kitchen.

'Now, tell me all about your week over in Adelaide,' said Grandpa Ken, collapsing into Specky's dad's favourite armchair. 'You made a bit of a mess of my lot from Western Australia. You bloody Vics always were hard to beat.'

Specky sat on the floor in front of the fire-place, and recalled the events of the past week for his grandpa. Unlike Specky's dad on the way home from the airport, Grandpa Ken hung off every word and bombarded him with a ton of questions.

'Really? You got to play on AAMI Stadium? Gee, that's a big ground.'

'How did your fitness hold out?'

'And you went and watched the Adelaide Crows train? Wow, how big is Andrew McLeod? Did you get to speak to him? What about Simon Goodwin?'

Question after question came Specky's way, and he loved it. He got to relive some of the great memories from the carnival. Grandpa Ken really knew his football, and Specky felt as if he could've talked with him all night long.

He was just in the middle of telling Grandpa Ken about his six-goal haul against Tasmania when his dad interrupted them.

'Simon, dinner's ready! Jack will be awake soon, and I'm sure you're looking forward to seeing him.'

'Give the boy a break, will ya, David?' said Grandpa Ken, before Specky had a chance to respond. 'Just because you didn't know a football from a basketball when you were a kid, doesn't mean we can't sit here and have a natter about one of the biggest weeks in the boy's life.'

'I wasn't talking to you, Ken,' said Specky's dad. There was a real edge to his voice, and Specky was surprised that he didn't call Grandpa

Ken 'Dad'. He tried to imagine what his dad would say if Specky started calling him 'David'.

'We eat dinner together, at the table, every night. That's the rule in my house and that's the way we like it.'

'It's okay, Grandpa,' Specky chimed in, trying his best to defuse the tense moment. 'We can talk about it later, plus I'm starving. I've been hangin' out for a bowl of Mum's vegie soup all week.' He jumped up and headed for the kitchen, leaving his dad and grandpa glaring at each other. Alice was right – it was going to take Dr Phil to sort out whatever was going on between those two.

6. mates and girls

'Hurry up, Speck! We know you're used to limousines and chauffeurs now, but some of us still have to walk to school.'

It was Robbo and Danny, impatiently waiting at the front door, doing what they did best – stirring and hanging it on each other.

'Yeah, coming!' shouted Specky, bounding down the stairs. 'See ya, Mum, Dad, Grandpa Ken.'

Specky joined his friends and they set off for school.

'Here he is – the man described as the "excitement machine" of the National Carnival. Ladies and gentleman, I present to you the future number one draft pick . . . Simon "Specky" Magee!'

'Knock it off, will ya, Danny?' Specky laughed.

'Mate, great effort over there,' said Robbo. 'Danny and Gobba came over to my house yesterday and we watched every second of the game. It was awesome.'

Specky appreciated Robbo's support. He was a really good player in his own right, but there was never any competition or jealousy about the success that had come Specky's way.

'Yeah, but we were five seconds from chucking Gobba into the pool and locking him out of the house,' added Danny. 'He wouldn't shut up, and insisted on calling every second of the whole game. It was driving us nuts.'

Specky could picture it all. Ben Higgins – or 'Gobba', as Specky and his mates called him – lived and breathed football commentating. He was so good that he had won a coveted position at the Dennis Cometti Commentary School for up-and-coming young callers. It didn't matter what was happening in their world, if Gobba was around he would turn it into a broadcast.

For the next few minutes, conversation bounced all over the place. Specky soon found himself answering what seemed like a hundred questions.

'You're kiddin, aren't ya?' cried Robbo. 'Chris Judd actually spoke to you before one of your games, and you got to shake his hand? What was he doing over there and what did he have to say? Come on, Speck, don't hold back. I can't believe you didn't text us and tell us.'

'Well, you know how Carlton played Port Adelaide at AAMI Stadium last week?'

The boys stopped walking.

'Yeah.' They nodded.

'Well, they were staying at the hotel just up the road, and because Grub had coached Juddy when he played for the Vics in the Under Fifteens, he asked him if he could spare us a few minutes. He stayed for about an hour and it was unbelievable.'

'Man, you're so lucky,' sighed Danny. 'You got to talk to a superstar like Juddy! I'm a Pies man, through and through, but he's an absolute legend. Wish he played for us.'

Specky grinned. 'So, what's been happening around here?' he said. 'Did we win on the weekend?'

Robbo and Danny talked over the top of each other.

'Yeah, we got up by a couple of goals.'

'Robbo killed 'em. He kicked five goals.'

'Yeah, well, the Italian Stallion here didn't do too bad, either. He gave a couple of 'em to me on a plate.'

Specky laughed – Danny had christened himself the Italian Stallion years ago in reference to his family's Italian heritage and the name had stuck.

Robbo and Danny went on to recall the different passages of play from Saturday's game. Specky loved every minute of it. Playing for the Vics was great, but he really loved playing with his mates from Booyong High and he wished he hadn't had to choose between the two.

Beep! Beep! Danny pulled his mobile out of his pocket.

'Gee, she's a bit late this morning, Stallion,' stirred Robbo, smirking. 'She usually gets at least fifty messages in before school starts.'

'Yeah, good one, you big tree,' Danny said, as he read the message.

'Is that Maria?' asked Specky.

'Yeah, who else?' Danny groaned. 'She's killing me, Speck. I can't move without her wanting to know where I am every minute of the day, and who I'm with.'

Danny's thumb raced across the phone as he shot off a reply.

Specky looked at Robbo for an explanation.

'Booyong High's great love story is hitting rocky times, Speck. Seems the Italian Stallion is getting a little bit smothered by the Gladiator.'

Maria Testi and Danny had been an item for three months. She was known as the Gladiator because of all the athletic training she did. She was one of the State's best sprinters. Given that Danny, a rover for their school football team, was a good twenty centimetres shorter than the Gladiator, they certainly made an odd-looking couple.

'You can't talk, Roberts,' Danny snapped defensively. 'You and Tiger Girl are like Siamese twins, joined at the hips.'

'Yeah, well, maybe not for much longer,' muttered Robbo, suddenly not so keen to continue the debate.

'What do you mean, mate? You and TG fighting or something?' enquired Specky, not sure if he should push for more information. Samantha

Shepherd – whose nickname was Tiger Girl because she was obsessed with the Richmond Football Club – was one of his closest friends and he didn't want to get involved in any problems between her and Robbo.

'Nah, nothing,' mumbled Robbo. 'But this little dweeb won't be able to walk for much longer if he keeps this up.'

Robbo jumped on Danny and wrestled him to the nature strip. Specky grinned. The day had barely started and his friends were already sprawled on the grass – school bags and books flung everywhere. Robbo managed to sit on Danny and deliver a particularly savage 'typewriter' to the chest.

'Come on, I'm going,' announced Specky. 'I don't want to be late first day back.'

Robbo and Danny picked themselves up, collected their books, and chased after Specky.

Beep! Beep!

'Right, that's it!' said Danny. 'I've had enough!'

Specky and Robbo snorted.

'No, seriously, you guys, this isn't funny anymore,' moaned Danny. 'It's wearing me down. I'm laying down the law to her today.'

Danny turned off his phone and shoved it into his backpack.

'Yeah, sure you will, Stallion,' scoffed Robbo. 'As soon as you see her, it will be all, "Yes, babe, of course, babe." Face it, dude, you're fairly and squarely under the thumb.'

Specky found himself wishing for the days when girls hadn't even gotten a look in with him and his mates. Nowadays, it seemed that's all that occupied their minds.

But Specky's thoughts were interrupted by the appearance of a stranger making his way towards them – he was well-dressed, carrying a white plastic bag, and seemed to have been waiting in front of the school for them.

'G'day, Simon,' he said, holding out his hand and passing Specky a business card. 'Brad Dobson's the name.'

The card read:

Sports Management Australia
Brad Dobson
Talent Manager

Danny and Robbo read it over Specky's shoulder.

'Congratulations on your win in Adelaide,' said

the man. 'We at Sports Management Australia have been keeping an eye on you for a good twelve months now. We think you've got a really exciting future ahead of you, and your perform-ances at the carnival confirmed that.'

'Ah, thanks,' said Specky, completely caught off-guard and feeling a bit self-conscious.

'We'd like to make a time to sit down and talk with you and your parents in the next week or so about the prospect of my company managing your football career.'

'Why does he need a manager?' Danny asked.

'Football's a big business now, son,' said Brad Dobson, turning to Danny. 'Your mate here has got some big opportunities ahead of him and we can ensure he makes the most of them.'

Turning back to Specky, Brad Dobson contin-ued his pitch. 'I don't want to put any pressure on you, but if you could pass this card on to your mum and dad and get them to call me, that would be great. You don't want to miss the boat, champ.'

As he turned to leave, he handed the bag to Specky and grinned. 'I hope these will fit – it's just a little something from the team at SMA, to congratulate you on a great carnival.'

Specky stood there in silence as the man walked away. Then Robbo gave him a shove, 'What did he give you, mate?'

Specky snapped out of it and ripped open the bag. Inside, was a brand-new pair of footy boots – the same style that Shane Crawford wore in his last year of AFL footy.

'Woah, that's awesome,' said Robbo. 'They must be worth a couple of hundred bucks, at least. What happens if you join up? Will there be jumpers, tracksuits and runners as well?'

'Who knows?' shrugged Specky, not sure what to make of the unexpected encounter.

He was kind of excited to be considered by a talent manager, but he felt strange about being given a gift. Somehow, it just didn't feel right.

7. maths attack

'What are you gonna do, Speck?' asked Sanjay Sharma. The 'Bombay Bullet', as he was known, was one of Specky's team-mates. 'Are you gonna give his business card to your olds?'

'Not sure, really.' Specky shrugged. 'I haven't ever thought about managers and stuff like that. Maybe it's a bit early to be worrying about all that.' He had shoved the shoes in his locker. They'd have to stay there until he decided what to do about Brad Dobson.

'Hey, legend! Good to see you back mixing with us normal people.' Specky turned to see Tiger Girl walking into the room along with Danny's girlfriend, Maria. She sat down next to Specky. 'You were fantastic, Speck, well done,' she said. 'I watched the game yesterday all on my own so I could concentrate without any interruptions. It's nice to cheer for someone other than my beloved Tiges. So, how did you pull up? That WA player was huge.'

'Hey, thanks, TG! Yeah, I pulled up okay,' said Specky. 'Just a couple of bruises here and there, but nothing too serious. When are you gonna give up on Richmond?'

'Get real!' she laughed. 'Richo has had another awesome year, and Trent Cotchin is just as good or even better than Judd. Oh, and did I mention that Brett Deledio has a Best and Fairest to his name? Anyway, when are *you* gonna decide who your favourite team is? I recommend Richmond!'

Specky had always received a lot of ribbing from his friends when it came to his support for a number of AFL clubs. Ever since he was little, he had barracked for five teams. He had a personal connection with each team and he couldn't choose just one. They included Essendon, because when he was younger he'd had a fascination for jet bombers; Brisbane because his school team was also the Lions; Collingwood and Sydney because his best mates

Robbo and Danny followed them; and finally, West Coast, because of Grandpa Ken – a one-eyed Eagles fan from Perth.

Now, as a teenager, Specky knew that this was kind of absurd, but he still wasn't ready to just pick one. It had always been the love of the game for him and not just the love of one particular team.

'Fair call!' He grinned. 'I might just follow the Eagles for the next few weeks, since my grandpa is in town.'

Specky loved that he could talk footy with TG. Sometimes, he thought, she really felt like one of the boys.

'I so want to go and watch you play on the MCG on Grand Final Day,' she added. 'I'll scream my head off. What's the go with tickets? I've put my name down in the ballot, and Dad's keeping his eye out for me, but any chance you can get me one?'

Before Specky could answer, Robbo jumped in, sounding a bit offended. 'I said I'd try and get some tickets for us, Sam.'

'Yeah, I know, Josh, but I just thought that the Speckster here might have more of a chance.'

Specky noticed that Robbo seemed hurt by TG's comments.

'Well, I'll be there and I'll have the best seat in the house,' chimed in Gobba, with a huge grin plastered across his face.

'Don't tell me you made it to the final four?' asked Specky, happy to move the conversation away from Grand Final tickets and anything to do with TG and Robbo's relationship.

'Yep, I sure did! The four finalists from the Dennis Cometti School all get to commentate one quarter of your game, Speck. How awesome is that? And the best caller of that game, the winning commentator, will be awarded the Cork in the Ocean trophy. I'm so gonna go for it!'

Everyone congratulated Gobba, patting him on the back – they were all just as excited about Gobba's budding commentary career as they were about Specky's football feats.

'Well, if we're all making announcements, then I've got one, too.' Derek 'Screamer' Johnson, who was sitting behind them, leant forward to join the conversation. 'I'm leaving Booyong High at the end of this term and moving to Sydney. I won a scholarship to attend Eckert

School of Music. It's the best in the country. I'm stoked!'

As his classmates congratulated Screamer, Specky couldn't help thinking about how much Screamer had changed recently. He used to be a hard-hitting bully who excelled in footy and beating people up, but ever since he had focused on his other passion, playing the piano, it was almost as if he were a different kid.

'Look out, Speck. If Screamer is moving to Sydney he'll move in on your girl. If he hasn't already,' stirred Danny.

'Christina's not my girl,' Specky said, even though it was difficult for him to say out loud. 'She can do what she likes.'

'You're a jerk, Castellino,' Screamer snapped, making a fist. 'Don't make me teach you a lesson before I leave.'

Perhaps he wasn't so different! Specky thought.

'Oooh, I'm really scared,' said Danny. 'What're you gonna do? Torture me by making me listen to one of your concerts?'

Specky sometimes wondered if Danny's mouth was attached to his brain. It was always getting him in trouble. Screamer lunged across his desk at Danny, but the Gladiator jumped between them.

'You lay one finger on him and I'll crush those scholarship-winning fingers for you!'

Specky knew Screamer well enough to know that even he wouldn't contemplate hitting a girl, but even if he would, Maria could definitely hold her own. She was stronger and tougher than most of the Booyong High boys put together. Danny looked relieved that his 'bodyguard' was there to protect him.

'THAT'S QUITE ENOUGH NOISE COMING FROM THIS ROOM!'

Everyone spun around and faced the front of the classroom. The chatter stopped immediately. Having had three emergency Maths teachers this term, today was the day that Specky and his classmates were to meet the new permanent appointment.

In marched a tall, solid, silver-haired man with the presence and confidence of an army general.

'Mr Rutherford's my name, and you will all learn very quickly that you don't talk in my class until I invite you to. Now take your seats. I've got a nice little surprise to start off your week.'

Specky and Robbo exchanged looks as if to say, 'What are we in for?'

As the students settled into their chairs, Maria turned to Danny and whispered, 'You're welcome, by the way. Screamer cheeses me off. Hey, where's that pen I bought you last week? It matches mine, you know.'

Danny's face flushed bright red, and others in earshot giggled at the love-struck Maria.

'Young lady, you obviously have trouble with your hearing,' roared the new teacher. 'Pack up your books and come and sit in front of me.'

'But I always sit next to Danny,' protested Maria. 'I *need* to sit next to him.'

'You *need* to button your lips,' snapped Mr Rutherford.

Devastated, Maria did as she was told and moved to the front of the room.

'Now,' continued Mr Rutherford, 'I can't very well help you become Maths geniuses if I don't know what you're capable of. So, to help me get an understanding of your capabilities, I have a test for you to take this morning.'

Groans rippled through the classroom.

'Did he just say what I think he said?' muttered

Paul 'Smashing Sols' Solomon, another one of Specky's Booyong team-mates.

'Am I going to have to have everyone's hearing tested?' replied Mr Rutherford, his face hardening. 'Pass these around. You've got five minutes to read through the paper, and then forty minutes to complete the exam. Your time starts now.'

Specky couldn't believe this was happening. He'd had a week and a half off school for the National Carnival and he was hoping to be able to ease back into schoolwork. The last thing he'd expected, or felt like doing, was taking a test in his least favourite subject.

After ten minutes of everyone wrestling with the first few questions, Mr Rutherford's voice boomed out from the front of the class.

'Magee? Simon Magee? Could you put your hand up, please, and identify yourself?'

Specky self-consciously raised his hand.

'Ah, so you're our Victorian football hero, are you? Okay, get back to it. I just wanted to put a face to the name. I hope you're as good at Maths as you are at football,' he added, ominously.

During lunch break, the only topic of conversation between Specky and his friends was the new Maths teacher.

'What a jerk,' moaned Robbo.

'Yeah, who springs a test on their very first day?' complained Danny. 'Talk about not winning any popularity votes.'

'Yeah, I wasn't prepared for that,' grumbled Specky.

'Don't worry about it, boys,' grinned TG, one of the few who had taken the test in her stride. 'I'm sure he's not that bad. He just wanted to let us know who's boss.'

'Yeah, well, I'm glad we only have to put up with him for couple of lessons a week,' said Gobba, who for once had lost the urge to turn the conversation into some form of commentary.

Specky agreed. 'Good point, Gob,' he nodded. 'I've got a feeling that the less I see of good old Mr Rutherford, the better off I'll be.'

Just then the school PA system crackled to life:

'Attention, students! Could all members of the Under-Fifteen Football Team please make their way to the school gymnasium for an important announcement. That's all members of the Under-Fifteen Football

Team to make their way to the school gymnasium for an important announcement. Thank you.'

Specky and his team-mates exchanged curious looks before heading to the gym.

'Wonder what this is all about.'

'Dunno, Gobba,' shrugged Danny. 'Maybe it has to do with the training schedule for the finals.'

Everyone filed into the gym and sat down at the front of the basketball court. Coach Pate waited for them to settle. She had coached the Lions for several years and had led them to a couple of Premierships. They had all been a little skeptical at first about having a female coach, but she was passionate about footy and had won the respect of the whole team.

'Right, boys, thanks for arriving so promptly,' she said matter-of-factly. 'I wish you could be this quick for our school assemblies! I'll get to the reason for this meeting in a minute, but first a couple of announcements. Congratulations, of course, to Simon Magee for his mighty effort for Victoria at the National Championships. We're all very proud of you, Simon.'

A spontaneous round of applause echoed off the gymnasium walls.

'Secondly, I would like to welcome a new student to our school.'

Everyone turned their attention to the boy sitting next to Specky.

'Kyle, if you could stand up, please,' said Coach Pate.

The tall, slightly built boy slowly stood up, not really making eye contact with anyone.

Coach Pate continued. 'Kyle is from Queensland and has moved down with his family because his father has taken on a new job. You will all be pleased to know that he is a very talented footballer and will be joining us for training tomorrow night.'

Again the boys clapped, although not quite as enthusiastically as they had for Specky.

'Unfortunately,' Coach Pate continued, 'I have other news. And I haven't been looking forward to this moment. I won't be in charge of training tomorrow night . . .' Specky, Danny and Robbo exchanged confused looks '. . . as I'm afraid that I'm leaving Booyong High. Actually, I've resigned and I'll be leaving next week. It's so sudden because I'll be heading to Italy to join my fiancé, who has been posted there for the next two years.'

Specky and his team-mates all began talking at once. It was so close to finals time – no one could believe they wouldn't have their trusted coach to lead them to victory. Coach Pate looked as if she was almost in tears. Specky was gob-smacked. His favourite teacher was leaving!

'Please, boys, settle down,' Coach Pate said, trying to compose herself. 'I will be around for this weekend's game to say a proper goodbye and, of course, to help the new coach settle in. But because of the rushed circumstances and my time constraints, the new coach will start immediately. As of today.'

'So, okay then, who's our new coach?' Danny called out.

'Well, I was just getting to that. But nice to know you're moving on already, Danny,' Coach Pate added wryly. 'Your new coach is . . . well, perfect timing. Here he is now.'

They all heard the gym door opening and turned to see who it was. There was a stunned silence and Specky's jaw dropped. It was their Maths teacher, Mr Rutherford.

As Mr Rutherford crossed the gym, Specky leant over to Kyle, the new boy, and whispered,

'We had this bloke today, first period. He's the teacher from hell. A dead-set nightmare.'

'A round of applause, please,' said Coach Pate, 'for your new coach, Mr Rutherford, who also happens to be Kyle's father.'

Specky wished he could sink into the floor.

8. spelling it out

Specky turned up for his first training session with their new football coach. He couldn't believe Coach Pate would no longer be in charge of the Booyong Lions.

Specky had enjoyed a fantastic relationship with Coach Pate. Like many of his favourite coaches in the AFL – Paul Roos, Bomber Thompson, Rodney Eade – she was someone who understood the strengths and weaknesses of the team and was able to get the best out of everyone.

Specky's thoughts turned to Mr Rutherford. He grimaced at the thought of his new coach, but tried to keep an open mind.

Right, he thought, as he pulled on his boots and made his way to the oval. Don't make your mind up on this guy after just one encounter.

'Okay, boys!' announced Mr Rutherford. 'Coach Pate has done a magnificent job with this team over the past few years, and I don't intend to let all that hard work go to waste. With the finals upon us I'm not going to make any drastic changes, but you'll all learn pretty quickly what I do and don't like. Now, go and warm up and let's get underway.'

As Specky started to jog two warm-up laps, the new coach called out for him and Paul Solomon.

'You two head over to the water station and start filling those water bottles,' he ordered. 'I'll get to you when I have a chance.'

Specky and 'Smashing Sols' stopped in their tracks, and gradually the rest of the team slowed and then stopped running too, wondering what was going on.

'What are you all doing?' hollered Mr Rutherford. 'If your name is not Magee or Solomon then you better darn well finish those two laps quick smart or I'll fill this side up with Year Seven and Eight kids who will.'

Startled, the rest of the team scurried off.

'What the? What's going on, Speck?' asked Sols, totally confused.

'I dunno mate,' Specky replied as he made a beeline for Mr Rutherford. 'But I'm going to find out.'

'Um, excuse me, Mr Rutherford, why aren't we –'

'Mr Magee, have you lost the ability to understand English? I have given you and Mr Solomon a clear instruction,' Mr Rutherford barked. 'Go and fill the water bottles, and when there is a break in training, bring them out and pass them around to your team-mates. And then go and fill them up again.'

'What?' said Specky. 'But I have to train. The finals are coming up and –'

'You have to do as you're told, Magee. The two of you can see me after training. Now, hurry up and fill those bottles.' Mr Rutherford blew his whistle and jogged over to the rest of the group.

'What did he say, Speck?' asked Sols, as the two slowly made their way to the boundary.

Specky had never felt so frustrated and embarrassed, but he knew what a hothead Sols could be so he tried to seem calm about it. He shrugged. 'Dunno, mate. He's going to talk to us after training. Now, give us a hand and fill up these bottles, will ya?'

'But, Speck! The finals are coming up, mate. And you're a bloody Victorian player. He can't do this to you – to us! This sucks! I'm not gonna stay here and fill water bottles. What a jerk . . .'

Sols was one of the toughest kids in Specky's team. While he was a fair player, he did have a temper, and Specky could see that it was starting to boil over.

'Come on, mate, settle down,' said Specky. 'Let's just do this and find out what's going on after training.'

But Sols wasn't listening. He angrily yanked off his footy boots, shoved them into his bag, and kicked the nearest water bottle, sending it flying.

'Nah, stuff him,' he said. 'He can stick his water bottles. Coach Pate never treated us like little kids. And we've done nothing wrong.'

Specky stole a glance at Mr Rutherford and noticed that he was watching the two of them.

'Listen, Sols,' he said. 'He's obviously testing

us for some reason. You're not going to let him get to you, are ya?'

'Well, I'm telling you, Speck – he better have a good reason for us not training or I'm done.' Sols was still angry, but to Specky's relief he was starting to cool down.

'Okay, mate, let's grab those bottles. The boys are having a break and we better fill them before our new coach goes off his head again.'

Specky and Sols jogged over to the group. Everyone was stunned as Specky passed out the drinks. Here was their best player, who was starring for Victoria and about to play on the MCG, reduced to the role of water boy.

'What's the go, mate?' asked Robbo, as Danny, Gobba and the Bombay Bullet gathered around him.

'Dunno,' replied Specky, doing his best to keep his own temper in check. 'He just said he would speak to us after you guys finished.'

Specky's team-mates all seemed embarrassed as Specky and Sols handed out the drinks. All except the new boy, Kyle. And as his dad wandered off to set out some cones for the next drill, Kyle called out to Sols.

'Hey, you, bring us another drink, will ya? I haven't got all day! The water boys were much quicker at my old school.'

Sols looked ready to kill him.

'I've got it, Sols,' said Specky quickly. The last thing he wanted was more trouble. He handed Kyle a bottle of water.

Kyle shot a dirty look at Specky as he took the water in silence. Specky got the feeling that his comment at the gym the other day had made him a real enemy. And Kyle didn't seem like the kind of guy who would forgive and forget.

When training ended, Specky and his team assembled in the change rooms. Mr Rutherford stood at the front of the group.

'Now, I'm not stupid, and I know that all of you are wondering why Simon and Paul didn't train with the rest of the group today,' he said. 'The simple reason is that while I love football as much as the rest of you, I place a higher importance on school work. With that in mind, two of you failed the Maths test I set you earlier today. There are no prizes for guessing who those two were.'

Everyone whipped their heads around to look

at Specky and Sols. Specky couldn't believe it. He looked over at Sols, whose face was bright red. This was so humiliating.

'That's right,' added Mr Rutherford. 'Mr Magee and Mr Solomon. Now, I know you might think that this is harsh, and Simon and Paul probably feel embarrassed at the moment, but I'm doing this to make a point and to set the ground rules straightaway. If your school work is not up to scratch, you don't play football. It's as simple as that.'

There was uproar in the change rooms and the voices echoed loudly in the tiled room. Mr Rutherford allowed the boys to talk for a minute, and then called for silence.

Specky thought his whole world was caving in on him.

'So they're not playing next week?' said Robbo. 'We're stuffed without them. This is the finals. We need the best side! We need Specky and Sols!'

'Now just relax,' Mr Rutherford said, raising his voice. 'We all want Simon and Paul to play in our next big game. So I'm going to let them play this time because today's test was unexpected.

But make no mistake,' Mr Rutherford added. 'I am deadly serious about this. Both boys will be required to sit the exam again next week, and should they be unsuccessful then that will be it as far as football goes for this season. You attend this school to acquire an education, first and foremost, not to enhance your football careers, regardless of how talented you may be. One day, you'll realise that I'm right about this and you may even thank me.'

Everyone began to file out of the change rooms, with Specky shuffling dejectedly at the end of the line.

'Simon,' Mr Rutherford called. Specky stopped and turned around. 'I know that football means the world to you, but you have to find a balance between sport and your school work.'

Specky just stood there, not trusting himself to speak. He felt like a total loser.

But Mr Rutherford had one final thing to say. 'Okay, I know that you're feeling angry at the moment,' he said. 'If you study hard for this exam, there shouldn't be a problem, but I understand it's not easy, so I suggest you get some help. There was one student in your class who scored one hundred percent in today's test. It was Samantha Shepherd – I think you call her TG? If you're friends, perhaps you could set up a study time with her. I know you can do this, Simon. And I certainly want you on the team.'

9. full-on tension

'And here comes Jack Magee, the little brother of AFL legend Specky Magee. Look at him fly! And he marks it on the final siren! The crowd goes berserk!'

Specky's baby brother, Jack, gurgled and giggled as Specky waved a soft toy football in front of him on the lounge-room floor. After what had been one of the most humiliating days of his life, Specky didn't feel like doing much else after training. Mr Rutherford had shot him down and he was doing everything possible to get his spirits back up. Playing with his baby brother, he thought, was a good start.

'And Jack Magee thumps the footy through the big sticks and it shoots over Grandpa Ken . . .'

Specky looked up to see that Grandpa Ken had dozed off on the couch. He had been watching a lame game show on the TV. As Specky grabbed the remote and turned down the volume, he noticed that the house was unusually quiet. Alice was supposedly studying at the Great McCarthy's place, and their dad wasn't back from work yet. His mum was having a nap, since Specky was giving her a break from Jack. Having a one-month-old baby in the house meant that none of the Magees were getting enough sleep these days.

'So, did he win the car?' mumbled Grandpa Ken, coughing as he woke up.

'I don't know,' shrugged Specky. 'I haven't been watching.'

'Well, it's a ridiculous show anyway,' added Grandpa Ken, sitting upright. 'Can't believe I conked out like that.'

Specky turned back to Jack. He sensed his grandpa was watching him. There was an awkward silence. Specky wasn't really in the mood for talking. And there was no way he was going to mention that he had failed his Maths test and had a nightmare of a training session. He hoped his grandpa would doze off again.

'So, how was your day today, boy?' asked Grandpa Ken.

Specky sighed. So much for hoping.

'Yeah, good,' he fibbed.

'Yeah, good?' said Grandpa Ken. 'What sort of answer is that? How was training this afternoon? Big State champion like you – bet your school team-mates are over the moon to have you in their side.'

'Nah, it doesn't work like that – it's the team that counts.'

'Come on, don't be modest. I bet they love it. So, anything exciting happen today? Come on, tell your old grandpa.'

It was weird for Specky to hear that. After all those years of just getting cards at Christmas, having a grandfather in his life would take some getting used to.

'Come on! Talk to me! You moped in here like you'd just won the wooden spoon.'

Specky shrugged, but he liked that his grandpa seemed genuinely interested in his day and that he dropped footy references every chance he got.

'Something good must have happened today,'

he pressed. 'Gee whiz, I think it's a good day when I pee and don't miss the toilet bowl.'

Specky snorted. It was an image he didn't want to think about for too long, but it made him grin. It was the first time he had smiled all afternoon.

'Um, well, there was one good thing,' Specky said, as he gently tickled Jack's tummy.

'And what was that?'

'I was approached by a sports management company. This guy came up to me before school today and handed me his card.' Specky reached into his pocket and handed over the business card.

'This is fantastic, kid!' bellowed Grandpa Ken suddenly, startling baby Jack, who started to cry loudly. 'Well, you don't just let an opportunity like this pass you by. Let's call him now.'

'What?' Specky gulped. 'Now?' It was all happening so fast. He picked up Jack, and tried to calm him down.

'No time like the present! Seize the day . . . *carpe diem* and all that! Where's the phone?' Grandpa Ken got up off the couch, waving the card at Specky.

'Um, I think I should wait till my dad gets back,' said Specky. 'And I'm not sure I need a manager.'

'Course you do! And what would your dad know anyway? He'll probably over-think it, as he does everything, and before you know it, you've missed the boat.'

Specky felt uneasy about his grandpa's last comment. There was some truth to what he said – his dad did like to think things through before he did them – but he didn't like Grandpa Ken putting him down like that.

'Is everything okay, Simon?' Mrs Magee shuffled into the room, still half-asleep with pillow creases across one side of her face. She took Jack from Specky, and he immediately stopped crying.

'Sorry, Mum,' said Specky.

'It's fine. I needed to get up anyway and start dinner,' she said, checking Jack's nappy.

'I can make dinner,' Specky offered. 'I can make rogan josh, if you like.' Specky prided himself on being able to make a mean curry.

'Nah, let your mother get on with it,' interjected Grandpa Ken. 'We've got things to do.'

'What things?' asked Mrs Magee, looking a bit annoyed.

Grandpa Ken didn't seem to notice. 'More getting-to-know-each-other stuff,' he exclaimed. 'We've got men's business to talk about.'

Mrs Magee shot Specky a curious look before leaving the room.

'So, where's that phone?'

Specky's heart was racing as his grandpa dialled the number.

'Hello, Mr Dobson. I'm Simon Magee's grandfather, Ken Magee . . . Well, that's why I'm calling you. We'd be very interested to hear what you have to say . . . Yep, yep, okay . . . And who do you currently represent? Not just AFL players . . . really?'

Grandpa Ken turned and winked at Specky. Specky smiled. He still wasn't 100% sure about all this, but Grandpa Ken was pretty cool. He was starting to feel excited about the idea of having a manager.

'Well, very good. You'd be more than welcome to come tonight after dinner.'

Specky's face dropped. Did he say tonight? But what would his parents think? Before Specky could get his grandpa's attention to reconsider talking to his dad first, Grandpa Ken had hung up the phone. The meeting was on.

'Don't worry,' Grandpa Ken said. 'When he gets here, you leave it to me.'

There wasn't a lot of conversation at the dinner table. Specky wasn't the only one who'd had a bad day. His dad had come home in a grumpy mood because his art gallery had lost the rights to exhibit a very successful artist, and Alice had had a fight with the Great McCarthy, something about priorities and not spending enough time with each other.

Specky's mum soon moved to the lounge room with baby Jack, leaving Specky, his dad, Alice, and Grandpa Ken at the kitchen table.

The sound of forks scraping against plates filled the dining room. There was a lot of tension in the air. At one stage, Specky glanced up from his meal and caught Grandpa Ken staring at his dad. He wondered what he was thinking. Why don't they get along? he wondered.

'So, Dad, I'm sorry about you losing that artist contract,' said Specky, trying to start some kind of conversation on a safe topic.

'Thanks, Si, but that's the way things go sometimes.'

'What sort of artist was he?' asked Grandpa Ken. 'A bull-dust artist?' He laughed at his own joke.

But Specky's dad wasn't impressed. 'I'd appreciate it if you didn't swear in front of my kids,' he said coldly.

'Kids! Come on. They're almost adults. And it was hardly swearing!'

'Well, swearing or not, kids or adults, don't use that language in this household.'

'Just trying to lighten things up,' Grandpa Ken said under his breath, but loud enough for everyone to hear. 'You never did have much of a sense of humour.'

Specky saw his father was barely holding himself back from snapping at Grandpa Ken.

'I'm SO outta here,' said Alice, getting up out of her chair. 'As if I need more stress and tension in my life.'

'Oh yeah, Alice, I totally forgot that everything was about you,' Specky said sarcastically.

'*Whatever*, dweeb!'

Alice stormed off, leaving Specky sitting in awkward silence with his father and grandpa.

DING! DONG!

Phew! Saved by the doorbell, thought Specky. But then he remembered who it was and started to panic. This was going to be bad – really bad. He heard his mum open the front door and then her voice calling for them.

Standing in the hallway was Brad Dobson.

Grandpa Ken barged past Specky's dad and welcomed the talent manager with a strong handshake. Mr and Mrs Magee just stood there looking confused.

Stepping inside, Brad caught sight of Specky. 'Good to see you again, champion,' he said. 'Let me know what you think of the boots and I'll grab you another couple of pairs.' Then he turned and smiled at Specky's parents. 'And you must be Mr and Mrs Magee. We love your son. We can do great things for him.'

'What on earth are you talking about?' stammered Specky's dad. He looked confused at the unexpected intrusion. 'What do you mean "great things"? I have no idea who you are, and

71

how you know our son. I do know, however, that now is not a good time to find out the answers to those questions.'

'Yes, it is,' Grandpa Ken snapped. 'This involves your son's future. That's why I called Mr Dobson here tonight. He works for one of the biggest sports management firms in the country and he's been good enough to give up his time because he wants what's best for young Simon here. Even if you disagree with me, it won't hurt to hear Mr Dobson out, since he's already here.'

Specky's dad looked like he might lose his temper, to Specky's relief, his mum stepped in and convinced his dad to hear Brad Dobson out. But they insisted that Grandpa Ken had to leave the room. This infuriated Grandpa Ken, but Specky could see that he wasn't half as angry as his dad was.

'Right, we're doing this only because my father invited you here and it would be rude to turn you away just because he has over-stepped the mark,' said Mr Magee, matter-of-factly.

'You weren't to know that,' said Specky's mum. 'But I'll be up-front and say that we don't believe for a minute that Simon needs representation.'

Without missing a beat, Brad Dobson launched into his company spiel.

'Our company represents some of the best athletes in this country. Over ninety percent of AFL players have representation. AFL is a business. And young guns like Simon here need guidance. What I saw at the final was a superstar in the making – the way he moves, his skill level, the cool head on his shoulders. We think he's going to be the hottest football prospect to emerge on the scene since Chris Judd and Nick Riewoldt. And even if you don't believe he needs it now, when the time comes for Simon to be drafted, I'd like to think you'd come to me first for representation . . .'

'Um, you can stop right there, Mr Dobson.' Specky's father had heard enough. 'Simon, if you wouldn't mind going to your room while I see Mr Dobson out.'

Specky stood, and awkwardly shook hands with the manager. He left the lounge room, but he stopped just outside the door. It was amazing to hear someone talking as if he was definitely going to play in the AFL one day. Even though he wasn't sure he liked the look of Brad Dobson, it was hard not to be flattered into believing everything he said. Specky knew it wasn't right to eavesdrop, but he couldn't help himself – this was his future they were talking about.

'Mr Dobson, let me get one thing very clear here,' Specky heard his father say. 'You will not approach my son again, ever, without first contacting his mother or me, and you are not to meet with him without both of us present. Okay?'

'Yeah, yeah, I'm hearing you, Dave. You don't mind if I call you Dave, do you?'

'Yes, I do.'

'Okay, sure. But let me give you a few days to think things over and I'll be back in touch for your answer. I'll get working on the paperwork, just in case, shall I?'

'We'll ring you, if we ever feel Simon needs your assistance,' replied Mrs Magee.

'We want to start moving on a plan for Simon,' Mr Dobson pressed. 'Got some big sponsorships all ready to go. A couple of the big teen-sports clothing companies and a major shoe brand are beating our door down wanting to throw stuff at him. I'm telling you, Dave, we'll make him a fortune.'

Specky sprinted upstairs as he heard his father and Brad Dobson make their way into the hallway.

'We're not giving up on your son, Dave. We're here for him.'

Specky peeked from behind his bedroom door and watched his father show the manager to the front door.

'Mr Dobson, I'm not completely familiar with the role of a sports manager, but if there ever comes a time where Simon does require one, you can be assured that providing him with a free pair of football boots will be very low on the qualities that we will be seeking. Goodbye, Mr Dobson.'

'What? Were they the wrong size?' echoed the sports manager's voice from the other side of the door.

'Well, what did he say? Are you going to sign with him?' asked Grandpa Ken, hurriedly limping down the stairs.

'This has nothing to do with you,' said Mr

Magee. 'And I don't appreciate you inviting strangers into my home. That man should never have approached Simon directly – it's totally unprofessional.'

Specky ventured out of his room only to find himself once again smack in the middle of his father and grandfather eyeing each other off. It was definitely no fun being caught between these two.

'Fair call,' said Grandpa Ken, turning to look at Specky. 'But can you blame me for taking it seriously? That boy is a superstar and it looks to me like you're getting in the way of him fulfilling his dream.'

'What? How dare you!' Mr Magee seemed calm, but Specky knew that tone in his dad's voice – it meant that he was so furious he was trying not to shout. He was very glad he wasn't the one in trouble, but he was worried. What if his dad kicked Grandpa Ken out of the house? Specky felt like he'd only just got to know him. If he left now, he might not see his grandpa for another ten years.

'Um, Dad, it's okay! I'm not so sure about that dude anyway – major creep factor going on –

I didn't like how he tried to buy us with free stuff and big-noted himself,' he said, trying to defuse the situation. 'And, Grandpa, Dad's not holding me back. He's always been there for me.'

'Yeah, well, I'm sorry, mate. It's just that your father doesn't understand what it is to be good at sports. He and his brother were never interested in that sort –'

'Well, I was wondering when you were going to drag that out again,' interrupted Mr Magee. 'Heard it all my life, so I shouldn't be surprised to hear it again after all these years. I thought after Mum passed away that you would've let it go.'

'You leave your mother out of it,' Grandpa Ken snarled through clenched teeth. 'You boys will never understand what it was like.'

Specky was desperate for a way to break the full-on tension, but he had no idea what they were talking about. Thankfully, Jack started crying upstairs and his mother appeared at the top of the stairs.

'Ken! David! Please?' she whispered loudly. 'I'm trying to put Jack to sleep.'

Silence fell and Mr Magee motioned for

Specky to go to his room. Specky walked off before his dad could change his mind. But it wasn't long before they started up again.

'Why are you really here?' he heard his dad say.

'I told ya,' Grandpa Ken replied. 'I've come to see my new grandchild.'

By the time Specky reached his room he heard doors slamming shut.

Beep! Beep!

Specky grabbed his mobile to read the text message. It read:

> *Robbo told me about what happened at training – sorry. I can help with the test. After school at my place 2morrow? TG x*

Specky sighed. For one brief moment he'd managed to forget about the test. He decided to go to bed early – the day couldn't end quickly enough.

10. one of the boys?

'Simon! So nice to see you. Come in!'

'Hi, Mrs Shepherd,' said Specky, as he followed her into the house. He had sprinted most
of the way there. In the lead-up to the final he
had decided to get exercise in whenever he
could. 'Is TG home yet?' he asked.

'She is – she's in her room. SAMANTHA!
SIMON'S HERE!' Mrs Shepherd called down
the hallway. 'Can I get you anything, Simon?
A drink? A sandwich? You look like you've been
running. SAMANTHA!'

'Um, just a water. Thanks, Mrs S.'

Specky waited in the hallway as Mrs Shepherd
went off to the kitchen. Music blared from the
far end of the house. He smiled. No wonder

TG couldn't hear her mum.

'There you go,' said Mrs Shepherd.

Specky swigged the water in seconds. 'Thanks! I needed that. I've been trying to pump up my metabolic rate – to give my fast-twitch fibres a work-out. I try to re-create the same intensity I feel in my legs when I lead to take a mark.'

'Oh,' Mrs Shepherd said blankly. 'Well, good for you . . . SAMANTHA! Look, Simon, just go through, and tell her to turn that music down. What is it with you kids wanting to blast out your eardrums?'

Specky walked down the hall to TG's bedroom. The music was thumping and vibrating through the door. Specky knocked. No response. He knocked again, louder, but still nothing. He opened the door. There in the middle of the room with her back to him, TG was singing and dancing along to some pop track from her iPod dock.

'Hey, TG!' yelled Specky, but she didn't hear him.

So Specky just stood there, not sure what to do. He realised that he hadn't seen TG like this before. She was totally lost in her own world, enjoying the music. She didn't look like the TG he knew – the girl who loved footy and was generally treated as one of the boys. She seemed . . . well . . . so girly.

Specky walked forward and tapped her on the shoulder. TG screamed at the top of her lungs and, swinging her elbow back like some martial-arts expert, she whacked Specky fair-square in the face. Specky fell to the ground, clutching his nose. It felt like Ricky Ponting had hit a six into his face.

'ARRWWW!' he groaned.

'What the hell?' said TG, turning off the music. 'What do you think you're doing, sneaking up on me like that?'

Specky mumbled that he and Mrs Shepherd had called out to her several times.

'You almost gave me a heart attack,' she said, sounding out-of-breath. 'Have I broken your nose? Oh my God! I'm gonna get you some ice.'

When TG returned and placed the icepack on Specky's nose, she began to giggle. 'Woah, I did a Barry Hall on your skinny butt,' she laughed.

'Yeah, well, I never knew that you were Jackie Chan in disguise,' said Specky, holding the icepack on the bridge of his nose. 'I'm lucky it's not broken.'

'Let me have a look,' said TG, moving closer, her face only centimetres away from Specky's face. 'It does look bruised. Hey – remember when we first met? We ran into each other and you thought you'd knocked me out. You totally freaked – it was hilarious! I guess we're even now!'

As TG had a closer look at his nose, Specky was taken aback by her eyes. He'd forgotten how green they were. And he'd never really noticed, until just then, that she had such long eyelashes. Or how pretty she was. In fact, lately he hadn't paid much attention to what she looked like at all.

'What?' asked TG, as she caught him staring.

'Nothing!'

'Yeah, there is. I can tell by that goofy look on your face. Have I got a zit or something?' she said, taking a step back and glancing in the mirror.

'No, no . . . um, no,' stuttered Specky.

'Then what?'

Specky didn't know what to say. TG was one of his best mates and she was Robbo's girlfriend – he couldn't tell her what he'd been thinking. He thought he could feel his face starting to go red. 'It's just that I hadn't noticed before that, um . . . that you had so many freckles,' he said.

'Great! Point out my imperfections, why don't you?'

'No! They're not bad. They're cool,' Specky blurted.

TG froze.

Did I just say that? thought Specky, his cheeks now definitely bright red. He could feel his heart racing as if he'd just sprinted twice around the oval.

'Um, yeah . . . well . . . thanks.' TG seemed even more embarrassed than Specky. Finally, she cleared her throat. 'We'd better make a start then,' she said. 'Maths fizz to Maths whiz – that's my mission.'

'Yeah.' Specky laughed nervously.

As TG brushed past Specky to get her Maths book from her school bag, she stumbled over his foot. Specky quickly grabbed her hand and pulled her back to regain her balance.

'Whoops!' she said. 'Nearly went over.'

'Yeah.' Specky smiled.

For a moment the two found themselves once again staring at each other. Specky was still holding her hand.

Just then, the doorknob rattled.

'Hey, you guys! Can you let me in? It's locked.'

It was Robbo.

Specky let go of TG's hand as if she had some highly contagious disease. And TG rushed to the door to let Robbo in.

'Sorry about that – this door sometimes gets stuck,' she said.

'I thought your mum got the latch fixed?' Robbo said, as he dropped onto TG's bed.

'Not yet,' she said, glancing between Specky and Robbo with a funny look on her face.

'Um, I better go,' Specky croaked. His mouth felt totally parched.

'What? You finished studying already?' asked Robbo, casually folding his arms behind his head. 'Why is your nose red?'

Specky didn't want to explain. He just wanted to get out of there as quick as he could. Nothing happened, he kept telling himself. It's TG – nothing *would* happen. But he couldn't explain the enormous wave of guilt rushing over him.

'Um, I got king hit by Jackie Chan,' he joked. 'So now, I've got a massive headache. I hope you don't mind, TG. Can we study another time?'

She nodded.

'Dude, you gotta watch it,' remarked Robbo. 'You don't want to be injuring yourself before the big game on Grand Final Day. Oh, and by the way, did someone mention Grand Final Day? Why, yes, I think I did – Ta dah! I have tickets!' Robbo pulled two tickets from his pocket. 'I told you I could get them!' He beamed proudly at TG. 'My old man came through with the goods, thanks to a business associate of his.'

Specky watched Robbo bounce off the bed and hug TG.

'Nice one,' he said. 'Well, I'm gonna head off . . . this headache is killing me.'

'Hey!' Robbo called after him. 'We still on for tomorrow night after school at your place? You, Danny, me, and a bit of Xbox action? Right?'

'Yeah, we're still on,' said Specky, catching TG's eye as he ducked out. 'See ya!'

11. splitsville

'Bring on the weekend!'

'Move aside, Speck – the Xbox kings are here!'

Danny and Robbo spoke loudly over each other as Specky answered the door to let them in.

'Keep it down,' said Specky. 'Jack's asleep. And I'm looking after him.'

'Where's your mum?' Robbo asked in a loud whisper.

'Does this mean we're not playing Xbox?' sulked Danny.

Specky explained that his folks had decided to go out for dinner and have a break from everyone. And that by 'everyone' they meant Grandpa Ken. So Specky had offered to babysit Jack, with the help of his grandpa.

'You guys can help me out,' added Specky, trying to make out as if it would be exciting. 'Look, it won't be for long. They've only gone out to the pasta place around the corner. They'll be home soon. But until then, I have to keep an eye on my little brother.'

His friends were not impressed.

'What about your grandfather? Can't he look after him?' asked Danny.

'Nah, he's asleep again,' said Specky. 'He sleeps just as much as Jack does. I s'pose that's what you do when you're old.'

Specky and his friends popped their heads into the lounge room to see Grandpa Ken snoring loudly on the couch. Then they made their way to the kitchen.

'So, where's your sister? Why can't she help?' Danny pressed, still hoping there was some way he could salvage their evening of Xbox fun.

'I'll give you one guess where she is,' Specky said, taking some juice from the fridge. 'She's at the Great McCarthy's, that's where! They're more married than you and the Gladiator, Danny.'

'Yeah, well, not anymore,' said Danny smugly.

'I broke up with her right after school. And I feel AWESOME! Can you believe it? I'M FREE!'

Specky turned to Robbo. 'Is this true?'

'Yeah.' Robbo nodded. 'But the gutless chicken didn't do it face to face. He dumped her on her MySpace page.'

'That's not true,' protested Danny. 'I was thinking of doing that, but then I decided to send an email to an address she only checks on weekends. I'm not that cold-hearted, you know. It's all good.'

Beep! Beep!

It was Danny's mobile. Terror swept across his face.

'Weekends, eh?' laughed Robbo. 'I'd start packing, if I were you. She knows where you live.'

Specky and Robbo watched as Danny checked his text message. It was from Maria. Danny read it out loud: *You're SO dead!*

Robbo cracked up and grabbed Danny in a headlock. Specky grinned, but he felt a bit worried for his mate – Maria Testi was not some-one to mess with.

'Rack off, will ya?' Danny said, pulling away from Robbo. 'So what! I can handle myself.

Love hurts and she's just in shock, that's all. She'll be over it by the end of the weekend.'

'Yeah, right,' replied Robbo, pulling a face at Specky.

'Well, I don't know what you're stirring me about,' retorted Danny. 'You and TG have called it quits, too.'

'What?' said Specky. 'Fair dinkum? When did she dump you?'

Robbo shrugged as if it were no big deal. 'She didn't dump me, Speck. I dumped her.'

'What?' Specky said again, trying not to sound too surprised.

'Yeah, look, I know she's great and all that . . .' Robbo said. 'But we just didn't really . . . you know . . . click.'

'Is she okay?' asked Specky, and then quickly added, 'I mean, are you both cool about it?'

'Yeah, I think so. She didn't freak out . . . actually, she seemed all right about it. Come to think of it, she was absolutely fine. It just wasn't working – you probably have more of a connection with her than I do, Speck.'

Specky nearly choked on a mouthful of juice. 'Um, you think? I don't think so . . .'

'Oh, here we go,' said Danny. 'It will never be another girl for me. It will always be my one and only true love, Christina,' he sighed in a melo-dramatic voice. 'And even though you live ten thousand kilometres away and are going out with my rugby-dude lookalike, I know one day we will be together again.'

'You're mental, Castellino,' snorted Specky. 'It's no wonder the Gladiator's going to kill you.'

'Yeah, she'll probably start with the "typewriter of death",' smirked Robbo, suddenly grabbing Danny. 'Grab his legs, Speck!'

'NOT AGAIN!' protested Danny. 'NICK OFF!'

'What's going on here?' Grandpa Ken bellowed, shuffling in. 'Turn it up, will ya? You're carrying on like a bunch of squealing girls. You woke me up.'

'Sorry,' said Specky, hoping they hadn't woken Jack as well. 'Um, these are my friends, Robbo and Danny.'

'Nice to meet you, lads,' said Grandpa Ken. 'So what are you all carrying on about? I bet you young bucks are fighting over some girl. No?'

'No!' All three of them said at once.

'We're just mucking about,' said Specky.

'Ah, I remember being the same age as you boys. I had ants in my pants. Did I ever tell you about the time . . .' But Grandpa Ken didn't finish his sentence. He had started to lean a bit to one side and was holding onto a kitchen chair for balance.

'What's wrong?' asked Specky. 'Are you okay?'

'Um . . . yeah, yeah,' said Grandpa Ken. 'Just a little dizzy. I think I got up too quickly.'

'You want to sit down?' Specky asked.

'Nah, I'm okay, lad. If you don't mind, I'm going to duck out for a little bit. Get some air. I've been cooped up in here all day.'

'Oh, okay then,' said Specky. 'But what about Jack? We're both supposed to be looking after him.'

'I won't be long. You'll be fine,' said Grandpa Ken. 'Besides you have the *girls* here to help you out. I'll see ya later. Ooroo!'

'Did he just call us *girls*?' said Danny.

'Well, he was obviously looking at you,' teased Robbo.

After Specky's parents returned, it wasn't long before they asked where Grandpa Ken was.

'Well, did he tell you how long he was going for?' asked Mr Magee, clearly annoyed.

Specky shook his head. His father muttered something about being irresponsible and marched upstairs in a huff, but at least it meant that Specky, Danny and Robbo got in some uninterrupted Xbox time.

Around ten, a little after Specky's mates had gone home, Grandpa Ken finally stumbled in.

'Where have you been? We were worried,' said Specky's mum. 'I thought you were staying here with Simon and Jack.'

'Look, I'm sorry. I got a little disorientated,' said Grandpa Ken. 'I hopped on the wrong tram and ended up in the city . . .'

From the lounge room, Specky watched his dad come down the stairs and bombard Grandpa Ken with questions. 'Not even a call?' he said. 'Why didn't you jump in a cab? Didn't it occur to you that we might be concerned?'

'I didn't have your number on me. And I only had a few bucks in my pocket. Look, I've got a splitting headache. I'm going to go to bed.'

Mr Magee was about to call after him, when Mrs Magee gently gestured for him to leave it. Specky was relieved. Grandpa Ken really didn't look very well.

Specky wished somehow he could convince his father and grandpa to get along – but whenever he tried to help he just made it worse. In fact, they seemed to fight more over him than anything else.

It was weird, Specky thought, but he didn't have time to think about it – he had the school finals and the biggest game of his life coming up, a Maths test he didn't know if he could pass, and something seemed to be going on with him and TG. It was all getting too hard!

12. lions v magpies

Normally on the morning of a game, and especially with a spot in the Grand Final at stake, Specky couldn't get to his school ground quick enough. He was nearly always the first to arrive. He liked to get changed into his football gear nice and early, so that his preparation was never rushed. But on this occasion he was struggling to find his usual enthusiasm.

He wandered into the change rooms as most of his Booyong High team-mates were pulling on their boots.

'Oh no, folks, it looks like Booyong's number-one man may have slept in this morning – he's looking a little sluggish.'

As always, Gobba was in fine voice. His running

commentary on all things, not just football, was tolerated – if not always appreciated – by everyone, but today Specky barely cracked a smile. He began to get changed for the Qualifying Final against the Yardley College Magpies.

Mr Rutherford was locked in conversation with Coach Pate as they huddled over the whiteboard, finalising the team for the first quarter. Smashing Sols was engaged in a warm-up kick-to-kick with the Bombay Bullet and Robbo, while Danny and their star mid-fielder, Johnny Cockatoo, handballed the ball back and forth to each other. Specky saw that the new boy, Kyle, kept to himself – stretching in the far corner of the room.

There was tension in the air, which was to be expected before a Qualifying Final, and there was an added feeling of uncertainty, given that Coach Pate was about to officially hand the reigns over to Mr Rutherford. If Booyong won this game they would go straight into the Grand Final. The stakes were at their highest, but Specky felt strangely detached. He'd normally be pacing around the room at this stage of the pre-match, kicking footballs and offering encouragement to his team-mates. Today, though, he copied Kyle's approach and sat quietly in a corner.

'What's up, Specky man?' asked Johnny as he sat down next to him.

'Nothing, mate, just trying to get in the zone.'

'Yeah, right, Speck,' said Johnny, a wide grin spreading across his face. 'Don't you know I can see right into your soul? You can't fool me.'

For the first time that morning, Specky cracked a smile. Alongside Danny and Robbo, Johnny had become one of his closest mates since he had moved to Melbourne from the Northern Territory the year before.

'I dunno, Johnny,' sighed Specky. 'Don't take this the wrong way. It's just with Coach Pate leaving, and Rutherford giving me such a hard time at training, and with the big National Final coming up, I suppose I wonder if it's worth it to run out for Booyong. If I don't pass that stupid Maths test next week I'm off the team anyway.'

'You do what you gotta do, Speck,' said Johnny. 'As long as it feels right. Just be sure you don't go against what your heart tells you to do. My grandfather used to say, "If you go into a game of football with doubts, you'll come out of it with pain." It's true, I reckon.'

Specky sighed again.

'I'll back you, whatever you do, man,' added Johnny. 'But I sure hope you're running out beside me in half an hour's time. Who else am I gonna make look good?'

Johnny slapped Specky on the back and went to join in the pre-game kick-to-kick.

Specky thought about what Johnny had said and began to feel a little better about the game. But at the back of his mind was the State match at the MCG. For the first time, he started to feel nervous – what if he was injured today and couldn't play? He tried to put the thought to the back of his mind as Mr Rutherford called for them to take their seats in front of him.

'Big day today, boys, BIG day!' he said. 'You all know the benefits of going straight into the Grand Final. I'm not going to take any credit for where this team finds itself. That belongs to Coach Pate here who has done an outstanding job over the past couple of years.'

A spontaneous round of applause broke out as Specky and his team turned to look at her, standing in the corner of the room.

'Three cheers for Coach Pate!' shouted Robbo.

'Hip, Hip, Hooray! Hip, Hip, Hooray! Hip, Hip, Hooray!' everyone yelled.

Tears welled in Coach Pate's eyes as she smiled proudly at the group of boys she had watched over for the past two seasons.

Mr Rutherford continued. 'The best way you can show your appreciation is by playing in the manner that your coach has taught you. Just because there's a different voice up here, doesn't mean that you have to do anything different. The fundamentals remain the same. I demand a fierce attack on the football . . .'

Mr Rutherford's voice began to rise and his gaze intensified as he looked around the room.

'Run in straight lines, keep your eyes on the football, and when it's your turn to go, regardless of your personal safety, I expect you to go – no exceptions.'

Caught up in the emotion of Mr Rutherford's delivery, everyone leaned forward. Specky had to admit that their new coach gave a great pre-game talk – he was really inspirational.

'Keep it simple, move the ball quickly and let's

play to our strengths,' added Mr Rutherford. 'Simon, I want you to start at centre-half forward, and Kyle, you go to full-forward. Those two will give us a target to kick to. Robbo, it starts with you in the middle of the ground. Give Danny and Johnny first use of the ball. Man on man in the back line. Tackle hard when we don't have the ball and run harder when we do have it. Now get out there and win this one for Coach Pate.'

The boys roared in unison and nearly crushed each other as they ran out the door. As the team's captain, Robbo proudly lead the Booyong High Lions onto the ground.

As he ran out, Specky noticed some familiar faces in the large crowd. To his surprise, TG was there with a group of her friends. She was waving at him with a big smile on her face. He liked that. Actually, he really liked that. He remembered how he used to look for Christina in the crowd and realised that, for the first time, he didn't miss having her there.

He waved back. But what about TG? Specky wondered. Was she at the game just to see him?

'GO LITTLE BRO!' screamed Alice, getting Specky's attention and breaking his train of thought. She was sitting beside the Great McCarthy and the Magees. He smiled at them, and he caught sight of Grandpa Ken underneath the scoreboard, standing on his own. He waved at Specky and gave him a thumbs-up.

Specky now felt the nerves kick in. This was it. Game on.

The Yardley College Magpies were a big team, and as usual Specky's reputation was well known. The Magpies' coach had dropped a couple of players back onto him, and during the first ten minutes of the match he had to work hard to get his hands on the football.

With only minutes before the end of the first quarter, the Bombay Bullet spun out of the pack at half-back and charged towards goal. He hand-passed over the top to a running Johnny Cockatoo, who took a bounce and looked up-field.

Specky doubled back and made his move towards the square. Kyle hadn't moved and was standing motionless, with his hands in the air.

He wasn't making any effort to follow the ball. Specky had been able to get a couple of metres on his opponent and Johnny booted the ball in his direction. The ball held up a bit in the wind and started to drift away from Specky.

Specky quickly summed up that Kyle was in a much better position to mark the ball, but still he hadn't moved. Specky sprinted back, and with a desperate lunge managed to position himself between Kyle and the Magpies' full-back. He knew he had to make out as if he was going for the mark, otherwise a free kick would be awarded against him for shepherding. He put both hands in the air and crashed into the full-back, the two of them tumbling to the ground – leaving Kyle all alone to take an easy, uncontested mark in the goal square.

Kyle spun around and kicked the ball through the big sticks, and took off in one of the wildest goal celebrations ever seen in the history of Booyong High.

He celebrated with a couple of cartwheels, and some high-five slaps to the crowd as he ran around the edge of the ground. Kyle did every-thing but thank his team-mates for the role they played. He didn't even look at Specky, who was slowly picking himself up from the dirt of the goal square and had started limping badly. He had received an accidental knee deep into his backside and it throbbed with a dull ache.

As the first quarter siren sounded, the Lions were ahead by two points. Specky and his team made their way to the huddle, with Kyle still carrying on as if he had single-handedly beaten six opponents to kick the goal of the year.

Robbo and Danny ignored Kyle, as he pranced around them fishing for compliments, and the rest of the team congratulated the Bullet, Johnny and Specky for the part they'd played.

'Unbelievable effort, Speck,' said Robbo. 'I thought Kyle was going to stuff it up.'

'Yeah, talk about ungrateful,' added Danny. 'He still doesn't know how he got that goal. What a peanut. Did you hear him? He said that's exactly how he used to play at his old school and that's why he's the best. He seems surprised that we're not all over him, like his old team-mates probably were.'

'Yeah, I can't work him out,' said Specky, as he applied an ice pack to his right buttock. 'One minute he's acting like some loner, the next he's showing off. If he loves his old school so much maybe he shouldn't have left. Anyway, we've got our work cut out for us out there. These Yardley College guys mean business today.'

Mr Rutherford's quarter-time address was short and to the point. He surprised everyone by not playing favourites when it came to his son.

'Kyle, you're being lazy out there,' he grumbled. 'You have to move, read the play as it's unfolding. Don't just stand there expecting the ball to come to you. And cut back on the celebrations, you look foolish.'

Specky noticed that Kyle tried not to look affected by his father's comments, but he obviously was. He gave his dad a filthy look, before grabbing a couple of orange pieces and turning the other way.

The next quarter was equally as challenging. By half-time, the Lions were trailing by five points.

Specky was again icing his corked buttock, and had found it more difficult to stride out as the game wore on. It was not a serious injury, but he knew it was going to slow him down.

'Well, folks, it's turning out to be a cracker of a game, especially for the great Specky Magee who's desperate not to allow his team to fall behind or else he'll be the butt of all jokes. And with the massive corky he's got in his derrière, you know it's just going to be one big pain in the bum!'

Specky shook his head. Gobba could find a joke in almost any situation. But Specky was a little worried. He kept thinking about how this injury might affect the game at the MCG, even though a 'corky' was unlikely to stop him from playing.

When the Lions took up their places for the start of the third quarter, Specky tried his best to put the National Final to the back of his mind, but without much success. There was a little voice inside his head telling him to save himself for the big game at the MCG, and despite his best efforts, it began to affect the way he played. Ten minutes into the quarter, he had yet to win a possession.

'C'mon, Speck, we need a lift from you, buddy,' urged Robbo as he ran past him to contest a boundary throw-in.

Danny managed to get a hurried kick out of the pack, and the ball dribbled along the ground towards Specky. Specky dashed towards it at the same time as the Magpies' captain, Toby Graham. Toby was shorter than Specky, but almost twice as wide. He was solid as a forklift truck, and had muscles on top of his muscles.

Both players set their eyes on the ball, with Specky getting there fractionally ahead of Toby. But as Specky bent down to pick up the ball he hesitated, remembering the hit he had taken from Mitch Mahoney in the game against Western Australia. As the huge player barrelled towards him, he took his eyes off the footy and started to flinch, anticipating what was surely going to be a massive collision.

The ball, however, bounced at right angles, allowing Toby to change direction, scoop it up and charge down the other end of the ground.

Players from both teams and a large part of the crowd went silent for a moment. They couldn't believe what they had just seen – Specky Magee, one of the most skilled and courageous players in the competition, had 'pulled out'. It was known in football circles as putting in a 'short step' and it was an accusation that no player ever wanted levelled at them.

Specky realised instantly what he had done. He wanted the ground to swallow him up. He prided himself on his toughness and courage, and had modeled himself on the likes of Jonathan Brown and Nick Riewoldt, players who never shirked an issue. With so much at stake there was no excuse, and the Yardley College players were not about to let him forget it.

'You packed your dacks, Magee.'

'How embarrassing was that, hero?'

'I suppose your Booyong mates aren't as important as your Victorian buddies, Magee. I bet you wouldn't do that if you were playing with them.'

Specky was never one to get involved in sledging, but this time he simply had no comeback.

The Booyong High runner sprinted towards him.

'You're coming off, Speck. Sorry, mate.'

To add to his humiliation, Specky was being 'dragged'. With his head down he jogged to the interchange bench, acutely aware that it was Coach Pate's last game, that all of his family was there, and that TG was watching.

Specky felt horrible and couldn't believe he had let them down like that. Even Gobba, who was also on the bench, didn't look him in the eye or make a comment. There was little doubt that this was one of the low points of Specky's year.

At the three-quarter-time huddle, the Yardley College Magpies led the Booyong High Lions by 23 points. Despite the heroic efforts of Robbo in the ruck and Johnny Cockatoo, who was playing a blinder, the Grand Final berth was slipping away.

The players were quiet as Mr Rutherford made his way over to them from the boundary.

'What do you think ya doin', Magee?' shouted Kyle. 'I'd heard so much about you when I arrived at this school, but you're nothing but a show-pony wimp, who's too gutless to put his head over the ball. None of my old team-mates would've chickened out like you did.'

'Listen, you big mouth!' snapped Smashing Sols, coming in to defend Specky. 'You've done nothing but take advantage of everyone else's hard work all game, so you can keep your opinions to yourself. And shut up about your old school while you're at it.'

'What are you gonna do about it?' baited Kyle, stepping up to Sols. 'Come on, I'll take you on . . .'

'Settle down, will ya?' growled Robbo. 'Focus on the game!'

'Yeah, we know which game Magee's focusing on and it's not this one,' Kyle said. 'We wouldn't have put up with it at my old school side, which is better than this crappy team!'

'You're really asking for it, weirdo,' barked Smashing Sols, raising his fist.

'PAUL! Step back now!'

It was Coach Pate, who had reached the team on the ground only moments before Mr Rutherford. Specky couldn't believe this was happening – because of him, his team-mates were about to come to blows.

'It's okay, Sols, he's not wrong,' confessed Specky. 'I pulled out. It was a weak effort. Simple as that.' He turned to Mr Rutherford who was standing there quietly, watching. 'Coach, I apologise. I don't blame you for taking me off, and leaving me there. I deserve it. I can tell you all, though, it will never happen again.'

Specky expected to hear Mr Rutherford agree

with him and bench him for the entire game. To his surprise, he didn't.

'There is not one player who hasn't felt the way you do now, Simon,' he said. 'Everyone has had a situation on the football field where, if they could have their time again, they would do things differently. It doesn't matter how courageous or tough you think you are, we've all found ourselves in Simon's position at some stage.'

'He's right, Simon,' said Coach Pate. 'Learn from it, and the embarrassment you feel now will be worth it.'

Specky remained on the bench for the start of the last quarter and saw his team-mates turn the game on its head. Danny kicked two quick goals. Robbo booted a booming major, from inside the square, followed up by goals to the Bombay Bullet, Kyle and then Danny again.

The Lions had turned a 23-point deficit into a 13-point lead. Specky watched with mixed feelings. He was rapt that they were going to win the game, but he felt pretty useless not having contributed.

Just as he was feeling at his worst, Coach Pate came and sat beside him.

'I meant what I said, Simon. Don't be too hard on yourself, okay?' she said softly.

Specky nodded, trying to look as if he were cool and calm about it all.

'And, look, I might not get another chance to say this before I leave,' she added. 'But you're an amazing kid, and you have a massive future ahead of you. I'm sorry I won't get to see you play the National Final, but I know that someday I'm going to see you play on the MCG – that's for sure. And when you do, I can proudly say *I* coached him . . . which, by the way, was an honour.'

Specky was taken aback. He didn't know what to say.

'And just one more thing,' she said, smiling. 'Have an open mind when it comes to Coach Rutherford and his ways, okay?'

Specky nodded again.

'Now, just in case we don't get to say good-bye – be good and take care, Simon.'

Coach Pate put her hand out, but instead of shaking it, Specky threw his arms around her.

'Thanks, Coach. For everything,' he said, hugging her tightly.

With three minutes of the game remaining, Mr Rutherford motioned for Specky to warm up. He was going to full-forward for the final moments.

The crowd cheered and applauded as he ran back on the ground. For a second, Specky thought he could hear TG yelling his name.

The game was almost over when Kyle took a mark, forty metres from goal. Specky's opponent ran towards the square, expecting Kyle to have a shot, leaving Specky all alone. All Kyle had to do was chip it over the man on the mark to Specky, who could then take an easy chest mark and kick a certain goal.

Kyle waited and waited, allowing the Magpies' full-back to sprint back towards Specky. Only then did Kyle kick the ball, but instead of keeping it low and drilling Specky on the chest, he kicked the footy way over his head.

Specky started to run backwards. He could hear the full-back charging towards him, but he refused to take his eyes off the ball. No one on the field would have blamed him this time – it was a horrible pass – but still he ran back at top speed. He raised his arms and took the ball in his hands, falling backwards as he did.

The full-back arrived a split second later and smashed into Specky's back, catapulting him forward, one knee striking the fleshy part of Specky's buttocks – the very same spot where he was corked earlier. He was in pain and the whole right side of his leg was numb but he got to his feet as quickly as he could. He was not about to stay down after the day he'd had.

Specky gingerly went back and slotted through the goal as the siren sounded. The Lions were through to the Grand Final.

13. cork

Specky woke up the next morning unable to lift his leg. His right butt cheek had swollen to almost twice its normal size. It would have been embarrassing if it weren't so painful. A corked buttock had been the diagnosis. The knocks had caused internal bleeding and Specky had set his alarm to go off every three hours throughout the night so he could apply a massive ice pack to the affected area to keep the swelling down.

Tired and in pain, Specky dressed and made his way to the kitchen for some breakfast.

'How are you feeling?' asked his mum, who was feeding Jack.

'I'll survive,' Specky said, through clenched teeth, not sure he believed it himself.

Moments later, his grandpa appeared.

'Need to borrow the car, Jane,' he said, as he poured himself a cup of coffee. 'Come on, lad, we're heading down to St Kilda beach. Gotta get you in the salt water to help reduce that swelling.'

'Ken, I'm not so sure. You said yourself you got a bit lost the other day, and besides it's freezing outside. He'll catch pneumonia.'

'Simon can be my GSP . . . GST . . . or whatever they call those electronic map things,' said Grandpa Ken. 'If he's going to be right to play in a week, we've got to get straight onto it.'

'He's right, Mum,' added Specky. 'The AFL players do it all the time and I need all the help I can get.'

'Well, as long as you're right to drive, Ken, and both of you take it easy,' said Mrs Magee reluctantly. 'Ken, don't keep him down there too long. And, Simon, take your mobile because if you . . .'

Specky didn't hear the rest. He and his grandpa were already out the door.

'I haven't said much about the game, but I will just say this one thing,' said Grandpa Ken as he drove off down Specky's street. 'You bounced back, lad, and I'm proud of you. You could have sulked after being taken from the ground, but you won back the respect of everyone at that game by showing your courage in the last minute. Now, all we need to worry about is getting that bum of yours right.'

As Specky and Grandpa Ken pulled up at the car park near the St Kilda pier, Specky paused before hopping out.

'What? You having second thoughts?' said Grandpa Ken. 'Cause I must admit, it does look a little blowy out there.'

'No, it's not that,' Specky said. 'It's just . . . well . . . can I ask you a personal question? You won't get upset?'

'Nah, course not,' said Grandpa Ken. 'There's obviously something on your mind. Spit it out!'

Specky took a deep breath. 'Well, I wanted to know what the problem is between you and Dad. Why do you seem to hate each other?'

'We don't hate each other,' said Grandpa Ken, awkwardly. 'We just see the world differently, that's all.'

'Right,' mumbled Specky, hoping his grandpa

would elaborate without him having to ask.

'Look,' sighed Grandpa Ken. 'I know you probably want some simple explanation. But life isn't always clear, or rosy for that matter. Especially when it comes to your father and me. It's complicated, lad. And to be honest I'm not sure if I really want to talk about it right now.'

'Okay, fair enough.' Specky shrugged, opening up the car door.

'Now, hang on!' Grandpa Ken called out, before taking a deep breath. 'I'm sorry if I've made it awkward for you. I'm not shutting you out, kid. There are just a lot of things that have happened recently to make me look at life differently, and there are things that I deeply regret. Like not being around more for my grandchildren – you're terrific kids, and I'm a selfish old fool who's missed a good part of your growing up.'

Grandpa Ken paused and sighed heavily.

'But it was never my intention to come and visit after all these years and stir things up with your father. Truly, it wasn't. And I am *trying* to get along – you've got to believe me when I say that.'

Grandpa Ken looked at Specky for a moment

and sighed. 'But for you, kid, I'll try harder. Now, let's hit that water!'

Specky's time in the cold salt water definitely helped. By Tuesday afternoon he was feeling a little better, but he knew there was no way he was going to be able to train with the Victorian team that evening. He wasn't going to miss being there at Punt Road Oval, though – cork or no cork.

As he hobbled into the change rooms of Richmond's home ground, the first person he bumped into was his friend Brian Edwards.

'Geez, Speck, you're walking like an old man,' he said. 'What happened to you?'

Specky explained what had happened in Saturday's game.

'Well, you've got a big job ahead of you, mate,' said Brian. 'A Grand Final with your school team and the National Final the following week at the MCG. What do you reckon Grub's gonna say when you see him? Do you think he'll let you play with your school team?'

'I dunno, mate. Do you think he'll ban me from playing?'

Before Brian could answer, Dicky Atkins, Skull Morgan and Bear Gleeson all wandered into the rooms. They were excited to be together again, and training at Punt Road Oval made it all the more special. The mighty MCG was only a hundred metres away, and with AFL finals in full swing the atmosphere around the world-famous stadium was electric. There were even a couple of television journalists out on the Punt Road ground conducting an interview with Grub.

'Well, here goes,' said Specky. 'I better get this out of the way. I'll see you after training.'

Specky made his way to the medical room to find Bobby Stockdale, the team manager. He had rung him straight after the game on Saturday, and told him about his injury. Bobby had been great, and given him strict instructions about icing the injury and recovery, but Specky was still petrified about facing up to Grub.

'How's it feeling, Simon?' asked Bobby, as he joined him at the physio's bench.

'Yeah, pretty good,' replied Specky, not wanting to raise any doubts about his fitness for the big game. 'It's improved heaps in the past few days.'

Just then, Grub's unmistakable voice got everyone's attention. He had finished his interviews and wanted to get training underway.

'Come on, you young guns! Stop standing around gas-bagging like a bunch of oldies at a lawn bowls tournament. Get ya bloody footy gear on and get out on the track.'

Grub's gravelly voice had an immediate effect on Specky's team-mates and they all sprung into action. Specky held his breath as Grub entered the medical room.

'Aww, Magee, that's not the greatest way to greet your coach,' winced Grub, as the physio and the doctor assessed the damage to Specky's right buttock. 'It's not your most flattering side, kid.'

Talk about embarrassing, thought Specky, his face turning as red as a Sherrin.

Grub ignored Specky for the moment and addressed the doctor and the physio. 'What's the verdict, boys? Are we going to have to amputate?'

'Not quite, Jay, but he has got some significant swelling,' said the doctor, laughing.

'It's not as bad as it looks,' protested Specky, desperately trying to downplay the injury.

'Yeah, well, I'm not asking you, am I?' said Grub. 'Go on, Doc.'

'Well, the bruising has come out, which is a good thing.'

'You call *that* a good thing?' said Grub, pointing at the massive purple, grey and yellow bruise that covered most of Specky's backside.

'It's a good sign, Jay. At least we can start some massage to try and move some of this bleeding. As you can see, it's started to track down his leg. That's why it's important to keep him off his feet for a few days. We don't want any complications with bleeding into his hamstring. If he does all the right things, I'm pretty confident he'll be right to play Saturday week. If he had a game this weekend it would be touch and go, and another knock on it would lay him up for three to four weeks.'

Specky lay there quietly, face down on the physio's table. After what had happened at the last game, he didn't want to be seen to be backing out or letting Booyong down. He knew he had to mention the schools Grand Final, but he was pretty sure Grub would ban him from playing. Just as he was working up the courage, Grub beat him to it.

'Well, you've got a decision to make then, don't you, Simon? Don't think me and Bobby don't know what's going on with our players.'

Specky put on a brave face and quickly sat up on the bench to face Grub and Bobby.

'I'll be fine, Grub. My body heals really quickly and I'll be running tomorrow and be able to train by Thursday.'

Grub, Bobby, the physio and the team doctor didn't seem convinced.

Specky ploughed on. 'I can ask our coach to play me at full-forward so I don't have to do as much work if that means you'll let me play.'

Specky held his breath, waiting for Grub's response. He had an uncompromising reputation and was not known to be overly sympathetic.

But Grub pulled up a chair and began to talk to him in a quiet, calm voice.

'Simon, I will never tell you not to play with your school team. You have made a commitment to them and they will be relying on you enormously. But I will give you a couple of things to consider when you make your decision.'

Specky's eyes were fixed on his coach.

'I won't take any player into the National Final who is less than one hundred percent fit. There's nowhere to hide on the MCG and we're playing a South Australian team that is desperate to knock us off and take the title back home. Now, you know that I want you – need you – to be available for us. You have an injury that will almost certainly heal in time to play. The game will be televised and every talent scout in the land will be watching and taking notes. And you need to know that you are also in contention for the All Australian team, which, if you're selected, travels to Ireland next year to play in the Youth International Rules Series.'

Now Specky's head was really spinning. He looked down at the floor.

'Should you decide to play for your school this weekend the chances of you being available the following week diminish greatly. And don't think you can bluff your way through a game and hold something back or take it a bit easy by playing at full-forward. If you go into a game with doubts, you usually come out with pain.'

Specky's head snapped up. It was exactly the

same advice Johnny had given him – and he had been right.

'So, I'm going to leave it up to you, son,' said Grub as he got up from his seat. 'Welcome to the big time, kiddo. Tough decisions are just a part of this caper and you're going to have to get used to it. We've all been really impressed by your attitude and maturity since you joined this team. I know you'll make the right choice again this time. But don't think for one second we're going to judge you, regardless of what that might be. We'll back you one hundred percent, whatever you decide.'

Specky gingerly made his way down to the boundary to watch training, having completed his treatment. Bobby joined him. The team was in top form and they were both impressed by the standard of football on display.

'You okay with everything?' Bobby asked.

'Yeah, I think so, Bobby. I don't know if I'll play yet, but I'm going to do everything I can to get myself right and hopefully train with the Lions on Thursday night either way.'

'Well, don't put too much pressure on yourself, mate. Just control the things that you can and the rest will sort itself out. You've got a long football career in front of you so don't make a bad decision now that you'll live to regret.'

As Bobby moved on to explain the science behind muscle tissue recovery, Specky was suddenly struck by a strange feeling that he was being watched. Over by the grandstand he noticed a familiar-looking man taking a great interest in what he and Bobby were discussing. It took a minute to place him, but Specky finally recognised the bald man he had seen at both Adelaide and Melbourne airports.

Who is he? thought Specky. Could he be another talent manager?

Specky turned back to Bobby to ask if he knew him, but when Specky looked back at the grandstand, the bald man was gone.

14. the test

The following morning, Specky shuffled into the kitchen just as the sun was beginning to rise. His mother was playing with Jack, who often woke up early and didn't go back to sleep for an hour or so.

'Hey,' Mrs Magee said softly. 'Why are you awake so early? We didn't wake you up, did we? We were very quiet this morning.'

'Nah,' mumbled Specky, opening the pantry and grabbing some cereal. 'I've got some studying to do . . .'

Specky realised what he had just said. He hadn't told his parents anything about how he had failed Mr Rutherford's Maths exam and been asked to sit another one. With any luck his studying would pay off, he'd pass, and they would be none the wiser.

'Really?' said Specky's mum. 'Studying? Studying for what?'

Specky had to think quickly.

'Um . . . did I say studying? I meant running. I've gotta get a run in.'

'What about your injury?'

'I'll take it really easy,' Specky called over his shoulder, as he limped out of the room.

As far as runs go, this one was very short and very, very slow, and by eight o'clock he was in his school library. He'd never thought he'd be looking forward to studying for Maths, but this time was different. He had organised to meet up with Tiger Girl.

'Um, sorry about moving our study time,' said Specky, pulling up a chair. 'State training was moved at the last minute.'

'Ah . . . the demands of being a superstar,' beamed TG. 'We mere mortals are just pushed to the background. But you won't be a superstar for Booyong if you don't past this test . . .'

Specky didn't have the heart to tell her that he might not be playing for Booyong anyway. 'Well, what are you waiting for, mere mortal?' he joked. 'Teach me all you know.'

For the next fifty minutes, TG took Specky through a revision of everything they had studied that term.

'So that means x equals thirty?' asked Specky.

'Yes, perfect!' she exclaimed. 'You have *so* got this now. I think you're gonna be okay.'

'Thanks, TG,' said Specky, sincerely. 'You're unreal!'

For a moment Specky just sat there, smiling at her. I've got to snap out of it! he thought. What's going on? All of a sudden he had strong feelings for TG and he couldn't explain why. He had always thought of her as a mate, even when he had thought she liked him. Was it just that his loyalty to Christina meant that he didn't want to admit he had feelings for someone else? But Christina was no longer in the picture and now Specky couldn't get past seeing TG as a girl . . . a girl that he liked. He squirmed in his chair. If she didn't feel the same way, it could ruin their friendship, and if she did, it could ruin his friendship with Robbo.

TG looked away and started tapping her pen

against the desk. Finally, she broke the silence. 'What's going on?' she asked, straight out.

'Nothing,' stuttered Specky. 'Nothing's going on.'

'Really?'

'Yeah,' said Specky, his mouth drying up. He had to quickly change the subject. 'So, um, I'm sorry about you and Robbo . . .'

Specky couldn't believe what he'd just said. Am I completely brain dead? Talk about a loaded conversation topic! Why couldn't I have picked something that has nothing to do with feelings? Like the latest footy tipping results or the latest Hangar McPhearson book? Or the weather?

'Don't be sorry . . .' said TG. 'I knew it wasn't going anywhere. We both knew it. Robbo's a great guy, but we didn't fully click, you know? Not like . . . well . . . like us.'

Specky was suddenly feeling very hot. Had the librarian turned up the heating?

DING! DING! DING!

Saved by the first period bell, he thought.

Specky quickly gathered his books and stood up, dropping some of his pencils on the ground. 'I got this,' he stuttered nervously, as he bent down to pick them up. 'Thanks again for your help. Catch ya later!'

Specky couldn't scurry out of the library fast enough.

'Good luck!' TG called out after him.

Specky glanced over his shoulder to see her grinning like the Cheshire cat.

Specky arrived several minutes late for the Maths test, thanks to a last-minute toilet stop. Nerves had set in. Sols was already seated and had started, and Mr Rutherford looked far from impressed.

'Right, Magee,' he growled. 'Obviously, this isn't important to you. I don't tolerate tardiness, so I've deducted one mark before you even begin.'

'You can't do that,' gasped Specky. 'I just needed to go to the toilet.'

'Well, you should have gone earlier.'

'Um, I actually don't have control over that.'

'Don't be smart with me, Magee. *Two* marks deducted. Now get to it!'

Specky shuffled to his place two tables across from Sols and began his test.

'So, when do you find out if you passed or not?' Danny asked Specky, while he and his friends kicked a footy during their lunch break.

'I'm supposed to see Rutherford just before the bell goes,' Specky answered, as he handballed to Robbo. He didn't feel confident enough to kick. His injury was still troubling him.

'And the great Magee is sweating buckets, folks!'

'Yeah, nice one, Gob, but actually I'm pretty confident,' said Specky, as he watched Danny and the Bombay Bullet battle to take a mark. 'TG went through almost all of the same problems with me just before the test.'

'Well, folks . . .' Gobba added, 'as another school term draws to an end, the men of the moment – Simon "Specky" Magee and yours truly – will experience one of the greatest days of their lives. But before we get too carried away, questions must be asked. Will Magee pass his Maths test? Will he play in his school team's Grand Final this Saturday? Will he go on to shine for his State side and blitz the opposition in front of thousands on AFL Grand Final Day? And, most importantly, will I – the magnificent Gobba – take out the Cork in the Ocean trophy on that very same day? Well, stay right where you are, viewers, because all that and more is to come right after the break . . .'

Specky grinned.

'Hey, Italian Stallion!' Robbo called out to Danny. 'Look! It's the Gladiator and she's not happy. And who would be, if they were dumped by email?'

Specky turned with Danny to see Maria marching towards them.

'Looks as if you can't avoid her any longer, mate,' Specky said. 'Too bad she's a State sprinting champion, otherwise I'd say run for it.'

'Ha! Ha! Very funny,' Danny said. 'Well, I have to face her sometime. Here goes.'

Specky and the others watched as Danny jogged off to meet Maria. The time had arrived for him to face the music. Specky expected at any moment to see the Gladiator take a firm grip of Danny's neck with her giant hands and strangle him in broad daylight. But nothing happened. In fact, from where Specky was standing, it all looked very civil. A couple of minutes later, Danny returned looking a little perplexed.

'So?' asked Specky. 'What happened?'

'Nothing,' said Danny, dumbfounded. 'She said that she was sorry that it had to end like this and she wished me all the best.'

'That was it?'

'Yeah. She didn't scream or cry . . . not even the sniffles. Nothing.'

'Well, that's good, isn't it?' asked Specky, snatching the footy out of the Bullet's hands as he ran past.

'Yeah, I suppose,' sighed Danny.

Specky was about to ask Danny why he was so down in the dumps, but the lunch break was almost over and he had to see Mr Rutherford.

When Specky reached the staff room, he found Sols waiting there patiently. Teachers streamed in and out, totally oblivious to the two boys hovering by the door.

'I'm packing it, mate,' Sols croaked anxiously. 'But I think I did okay.'

'Yeah, me too,' Specky sighed. 'Did you ask for him?'

Sols nodded. Moments later, Mr Rutherford appeared.

'Right, follow me,' he said. 'We can use Mr Stout's office.' Mr Rutherford ushered the boys into the vice-principal's room.

'Mr Solomon, well done. You passed. Forty-one out of fifty. You may leave.'

Specky gave Sols a congratulatory pat on the back as he left the office beaming.

'Right. Simon. I'm a little surprised,' Mr Rutherford said. 'I thought someone who understands what it means to work hard to succeed would apply that knowledge to other facets of their life. Evidently, when it comes to Mathematics, you don't. You not only failed this test, but failed dismally.'

15. fragile

The news of Specky's failed Maths test hit the Magee household a little before dinnertime.

'SIMON! COME DOWN HERE AT ONCE!' roared Mr Magee from the bottom of the stairs. 'YOUR MOTHER AND I WANT TO TALK TO YOU! NOW!'

Specky appeared sheepishly from behind his bedroom door. How had his father found out so soon?

He shuffled into the kitchen to face his parents.

'I am hugely disappointed,' said Mr Magee, his arms crossed in anger. 'Since when have you been failing Maths? In fact, you've failed two tests in one week, we've been told.'

'Who told you?' Specky asked, slouching and looking at the floor.

'Your new Maths teacher, Mr Rutherford, called us to explain why he won't allow you to play in the Grand Final on Saturday,' said Mrs Magee, looking as distressed as Specky's dad.

'Well, what have you got to say for yourself?' asked Mr Magee.

'This sucks,' Specky said.

'Excuse me?' said his dad, with a threatening tone.

'I can't believe I failed that test, Dad. I knew every question! That jerk's got it in for me!'

'Mind your language, Simon,' warned his mother.

'Well, it's true, Mum! I know I'm not that bad at Maths. This new teacher hates me or something. Yeah, I failed that first test he sprung on us, but just by a few marks. That's because I'd been away for a week and a half and I was still a bit distracted, but this other test, it's –'

'So, you're blaming football?' said Mr Magee, cutting Specky off.

'No, no, I'm not. It's just –'

'Well, if that's the case,' continued Specky's

dad, 'maybe we have to review your football commitments and what it means to your over-all education. You know where we stand when it comes to school versus football, don't you? Simon?'

'Yes – school comes before footy, not the other way around,' said Specky, his jaw tensing up. 'But maybe footy does come first? Or maybe it should at least be on the same level as school?'

Before either of his parents could answer, Grandpa Ken stepped into the room.

What a disaster, Specky thought. He knew his grandpa would be on his side, but he also knew that meant his dad definitely wouldn't be.

'I can't eavesdrop any longer,' said Grandpa Ken. 'The boy needs some back-up here.'

'This doesn't involve you,' Mr Magee said to his father. 'Just give us some privacy, please.'

'No, I'm sorry, I won't,' said Grandpa Ken defiantly.

'Ken, please. This is between us,' added Mrs Magee.

'Okay, Jane, perhaps you're right. Perhaps this has nothing to do with me,' said Grandpa Ken. 'But for what it's worth, it isn't fair to stop Simon from playing footy. Football is his future – it's his career.'

'The nerve of you. You think we don't know what's best for our own son?' said Mr Magee.

'I wasn't saying that!' snapped Grandpa Ken. 'All I'm saying is that perhaps someone like you, with no sporting knowledge or experience, can't be expected to understand –'

'Oh, here we go,' said Mr Magee to Specky's mum. 'He's going to throw this at me again. If this is the reason you've come back, Ken – to bring it all back up again . . .'

Specky caught Grandpa Ken glancing at him. He knew he was thinking about what they had talked about in the car at St Kilda and his promise to try and get along with his son. He hesitated. 'I'm sorry,' he said suddenly.

'You're what?' asked Specky's dad, clearly taken aback.

'I said, I'm sorry. You're right. It's not my place to say anything. I'll leave you to it.'

As Grandpa Ken turned to leave the room, Specky saw him stumble and grab at a chair for support, just as he had before.

'Are you okay, Grandpa?' asked Specky.

Grandpa didn't answer, and then he collapsed on the ground – unconscious.

It was midnight before Mr Magee returned home, alone, from the hospital. And though Alice had gone to bed hours ago, and Jack was fast asleep, Specky had waited up with his mother to find out what had happened.

'Was it a stroke?' asked Specky's mum, softly.

'No,' Mr Magee replied. He sounded a little breathless. 'No, he has a . . .' He trailed off and then started again. 'He has a tumour. My father has a brain tumour.'

'Is he okay?' asked Specky, realising what a lame question it was as soon as he said it.

'Well, he's conscious again, but he's known he's had this all along. I can't believe he didn't tell me.'

Specky watched his father zone out. He looked totally exhausted. 'That's why he came here after all these years,' he said. 'He knew he was dying. The doctors say there's nothing they can do. It's only a matter of time. They couldn't tell me exactly how long he's got. Six months. A year. No one knows.'

Specky watched his parents embrace. He had never seen his dad look so upset.

And he thought *he* had problems.

The following morning at school, Specky was walking down the corridor feeling depressed. He was so distracted he didn't even see Tiger Girl as he walked past her.

'Hey, you!' She tapped him on the shoulder. 'I heard. I'm so sorry you failed,' she said. 'But I really can't believe it. Is it true Mr Rutherford won't let you play? He can't do that, can he?'

'Yeah, well, I think he can . . . and now my folks are on my case, too.'

'That's so unfair!' she said. 'I reckon you should get the test back. We can go through it and see what you got wrong. You answered all the questions right when we were studying. Besides, it might put you in Rutherford's good books. Hey, you look pretty stressed. Have been up all night or something?'

Suddenly Specky remembered that if anyone understood what Grandpa Ken might be going through, it was TG. Having survived cancer herself some time ago, she was not only sympathetic, but also knowledgeable. Specky told her what had happened the night before.

'Oh, Speck! Is the tumour malignant? Is he having treatment for it?'

'I'm not sure of the details. But I don't think the doctors can treat it,' Specky said. 'Dad says I can't visit for a few days until he's stable. Can I ask you a few questions about it all? But not now, that's a really good idea to get the test – I'm going to talk to Rutherford.'

As Specky turned to head off, Tiger Girl grabbed his hand and squeezed it gently.

'I hope your grandpa will be okay,' she whispered.

When Specky reached the staff room he found Mr Rutherford outside talking with another teacher. When he asked to look at the test to see where he went wrong, his teacher looked impressed.

'Sure! Now that's the attitude towards learning that I like to see. I'll be back in a sec.'

Mr Rutherford returned with Specky's Maths test and handed it to him. As Specky flicked through the paper, looking at all the incorrect answers, he noticed something really strange.

'This test isn't mine!' he said, looking up at Mr Rutherford.

'What do you mean, it isn't yours?' he said. 'That's your name written at the top, isn't it?'

Specky nodded. 'It is, but it's not even my handwriting. This is . . . this is . . .' Specky couldn't think of a way to describe how wrong it was that he was being punished for something he didn't do. 'This is grossly unjust!' he said finally, borrowing a phrase he had once heard on a TV law show.

'Really? *Grossly unjust?*' scoffed Mr Rutherford, crossing his arms. 'You're not trying to be funny with me, are you, Magee?'

'No, I'm serious. This isn't mine.'

Mr Rutherford's face darkened.

'Of all the stories I've heard from students, this one takes the cake, Magee. I know you're desperate to play, but this is bordering on pathetic. Read my lips: you are not playing on Saturday.'

16. reality check

On Friday afternoon, Specky went by tram to see a physio in the city – an appointment set up by Grub. He had treatment and a deep-tissue massage and then a twenty-minute warm-up on an exercise bike. Initial signs looked good. The tightness that had been restricting his leg for a couple of days was now almost unnoticeable. But the good news only made him dwell on not being able to play for Booyong – he couldn't stop wondering about his Maths test. Someone obviously didn't want him to play in the final. There was no other explanation Specky could come up with.

After the appointment, he tried to put his emotions aside by going for a run. He pulled on his runners, grabbed the footy out of his bag, and jogged on to the nearby oval.

Only five days ago he had struggled to get himself out of bed, but now Specky moved around the boundary line of the oval with ease, alternatively bouncing the ball in either hand. For the first time, the problems of the previous week started to disappear. Specky was in his element.

He did half a dozen stride-throughs from one end of the oval to the other, increasing the pace with each one, so that by the time he was on his final run, he was close to full speed.

The relief he felt, made Specky realise how much the injury had been playing on his mind. He started to kick the ball high into the air – running, jumping, and marking the ball above his head. He felt as if he were eight years old again, playing for the fun of it. He sprinted around the ground, kicked the ball to himself, dribbled the footy along the ground and gathered it again at full pace, and took running shots at goal from impossible angles.

After forty minutes, Specky had worked up a sweat, and in his own mind there was little doubt he was fit enough to play for Booyong the following day. He ran back inside the medical clinic and, as a precaution, had the physio apply a massive ice pack to his right buttock.

Specky sat there, running through what might happen if he lined up for Booyong in the Grand Final. Luke Hodge, the Hawthorn champ, went into the 2008 Grand Final against Geelong under a huge injury cloud due to his injured ribs, and not only was he able to play, he also won the Norm Smith Medal for best player on the ground. But Specky knew that if he played and got injured early, his team would be down to just twenty-one men and it would almost certainly rule out playing in the National Final. Specky was aware that even AFL players were confronted with decisions like this. He had once heard from one of the leading medicos in the competition that whenever there's doubt about the fitness of a player leading into a game the question has to be asked: 'Will I be compromised in any way if I play?' If the answer is 'yes', then the player should have another week off. But after his time out on the oval, Specky didn't think he would be compromising anyone if he went out and played.

Perhaps now he knew that his Maths test had been sabotaged, he could convince his dad that he should be allowed to play. If he could get his dad on side, surely Mr Rutherford would see how unfair it all was . . .

'Dad, Dad, where are you?' Specky almost knocked the front door down as he went in search of his father.

'Simon, slow down,' said Mrs Magee, as she chopped vegetables for a stir-fry. 'Your father's on his way back from the hospital. He'll be here shortly. How did you go at the physio? Why so excited all of a sudden?'

'It went well, Mum,' he said, as he gave her a peck on the cheek. 'Just need to talk to Dad, that's all.'

'Well, it's nice to see you in a good mood, whatever the reason. Before you talk to your dad, could you go and check on Jack?'

Specky's brother was lying on his back in a bassinet, reaching up to the mobiles hanging from the handle.

'Hello there, little champion,' said Specky. He reached down to tickle him, and Jack grabbed hold of his finger.

'Do you want me to pick you up, mate?' Specky said, smiling. But as he lifted him from the bassinet, Specky felt a sharp pain shoot through his injured buttock and down into his hamstring. It came as such a shock, he almost dropped the baby before carefully laying him back down in the bassinet.

Specky was stunned. He'd been so confident that he had overcome the injury that he hadn't given it a second thought on his way home from the physio. But he was beginning to realise that Grub was right – if he played for Booyong, he wouldn't be able to play for his State. Even if he'd passed the test, he couldn't have played for his school.

'What's up?' said Mr Magee, appearing at the doorway. 'Your mum said you wanted to speak to me. I hope it's got nothing to do with your school match tomorrow, because you know we've made up our mind. It's a painful lesson, but we think it's for your own good. You won't be playing in tomorrow's game, okay?'

Specky brushed past his father without making eye contact and headed to his room.

'I know I'm not, Dad. I know I'm not.'

Specky woke the next morning with the strangest feeling. His beloved Booyong High were about to play in a Grand Final and he was not going to be a part of it.

The only thing he could do now was get to the game and try to provide as much support and encouragement as he could. Without being big-headed about it, he knew the team would be stressing because he wouldn't be taking his place in the side.

One by one, his friends had rung him to try and figure out some way to get him back into the team. Specky had decided not to say anything about the extent of his injury. He was glad he didn't have to choose between letting his friends down and being fit to play the MCG Final. Whoever had swapped the test obviously thought they were hurting him, but they had accidentally done him a favour and saved him a very hard decision.

When Specky arrived at the ground, he saw Robbo, Danny, Gobba, Johnny, the Bombay Bullet and Smashing Sols huddled behind the change rooms.

What are they up to? Specky wondered as he made his way over to them.

'Shouldn't you be getting changed? You've got a Grand Final to win, you know,' he said, startling them. They all turned at once, looking guilty.

'Oh . . . g'day, Speck,' said Danny. 'We were just about to head in.'

One by one, Specky's friends broke off from the huddle to reveal Gobba, with one arm bandaged from the tips of his fingers to his shoulder. He was awkwardly trying to put a sling over his head.

Specky couldn't believe his eyes. Gobba looked up, saw Specky staring at him and immediately started to moan and groan.

'Oh, my arm . . . my arm. I can't feel my fingers. I think I've dislocated my shoulder.' Gobba's face was contorted and he was unsteady on his feet.

'Mate, what are you doing?' Specky asked.

'Oh, Speck, thank God you're here, mate. I'm

not gonna be able to play in the Grand Final today. I was putting on my jumper and my left shoulder just popped out of its socket. Oh, it's killing me. It does this all the time.'

'Really?' said Specky. 'Your left shoulder, you say?'

'Yeah . . . arrgghh . . . oh, it's killing me. I'd better go and tell Mr Rutherford. He'll have to let you play. Oh, man, the pain!'

'Just one thing before you go, Gob. If it's your left shoulder that's dislocated, why have you got your right arm bandaged up?'

Gobba stopped moaning and looked down at his right arm. That was it – the others couldn't hold it in any longer and burst into fits of laughter.

'You idiot, Gobba!' roared Danny.

'Talk about overacting, Gob,' laughed Robbo, as he struggled to catch his breath.

'If you're gonna be a great commentator, Gobba man, you'd better learn your right from your left,' said Johnny.

'I'm sorry, Speck,' said Gobba, as the boys composed themselves. 'It was Danny's idea. He said Mr Rutherford would *have* to play you if one of us was out of the side. And since I wouldn't be too fussed – 'cause then I could commentate the whole game – I said I'd do it.'

Specky turned to face his mates, touched that they had come up with this crazy plan to allow him to play. He knew he had to be completely honest with them – even if it meant upsetting them.

'Look, guys, I can't tell you how much I appreciate it. But I need to be straight with you. Even if I had passed the Maths test, even if I was allowed to play today, I don't think I could've. I'm still not one hundred percent and I couldn't risk anything happening before the State Grand Final next week. I'm so sorry.'

'What are you apologising to us for?' Robbo asked. 'Don't you think we get that, mate. You should have told us! We know you're the one who's got a chance at the AFL one day, not us. There's no way we're gonna get in your way. We want you to do this . . . not just for you, for us.'

The others all nodded in agreement. Specky was gobsmacked and moved all at the same time.

'Then I won't let you down,' he said with a huge smile. 'Now, you've got a Grand Final to win. So get moving!'

17. booyong's big day

During the build-up to the opening bounce, Specky stood to one side of the change rooms feeling detached from the action. Parents and friends had done a great job of decorating the rooms in the Booyong colours: the walls were plastered with green, blue and white streamers and balloons.

Having finished writing his pre-game notes on the blackboard, Mr Rutherford approached Specky.

'I know this must be hard for you, Simon, but I really appreciate your being here. It means a lot to the rest of the team, too.'

Specky muttered a 'no problem', even though he felt pretty useless.

'Anyway,' continued Mr Rutherford, 'with Coach Pate gone I could really use some assistance on the bench with the team board, if you feel up to it. It's your call, but it would really help us out.'

Specky had a decision to make. He could sulk and watch the game from the other side of the ground, or he could put his disappointment aside and do what he could for his mates. It was a no-brainer, really.

'Yeah, sure, I'd be happy to,' he said.

'Great,' replied Mr Rutherford. 'Let's see if we can't fire these boys up and win us a flag.'

Robbo lead the Booyong Lions out onto the field to the sound of wild cheers and car horns blaring. TG, the Gladiator and the Bombay Bullet's sister, Gita, had spent the previous night making a big banner for the boys to run through, and they held it up as the team charged out of the rooms.

Once the girls had rolled up the banner, Specky caught sight of TG waving at him. He and Mr Rutherford were on their way to the coach's box, and TG had just joined the crowd of Booyong High supporters on the sidelines.

Booyong High's opponents in the big match were the Tremont High Tigers. The record between the two teams for the season stood at a win apiece. The Tigers were a small side, but extremely quick, and boasted two of the best rovers in the competition, Ethan Miller and Vince DePaglia. If the Lions were going to win, they had to stop these two players.

Gobba took up his customary position on the bench – minus his bandages – and quickly found his voice.

Well, folks, if you can imagine the Brisbane Lions without Jonathan Brown or Carlton without Brendan Fevola, then you can imagine the dilemma facing Booyong today. Simon Magee can only look on as his beloved Lions set about the task of winning this year's Grand Final. Only time will tell if they can overcome this enormous loss . . .

'That's enough, Higgins!' barked Mr Rutherford, obviously unaccustomed to having one of his players provide commentary from the bench. 'We don't need you reinforcing negatives before the game. Just concentrate and be ready to go when I want you.'

Gobba was shattered – Coach Pate had always allowed him to commentate from the bench.

Specky wandered over to Gobba as Robbo joined Ethan Miller – who was the opposition's captain – in the middle of the ground, to toss the coin.

'Don't worry, Gob,' said Specky, 'just call the game quietly. Mr Rutherford's probably as nervous as the rest of us and isn't aware that he has the next Dennis Cometti in his team.'

Gobba just shrugged his shoulders, staring daggers at the new coach.

Robbo won the toss and elected to kick with the wind. Sadly, it ended up being the only thing Booyong won for the first half. They looked flat and lethargic the whole time and struggled to find a winner in any position on the ground.

As always, Robbo tried his heart out in the ruck, but despite winning nearly every hit-out, the ball was always sharked by one of Tremont High's nippy rovers. Ethan Miller and Vince

DePaglia were running riot, picking up posses-
sions at will, and between them they kicked six
first-half goals.

The ball barely entered Booyong's forward
line, and when it did, Kyle, who had been put
in as full-forward, was almost always caught
behind.

At the end of the first quarter, Mr Rutherford
moved Danny onto Vince DePaglia and Johnny
onto Ethan Miller to see if they could slow down
the two stars from Tremont. Unfortunately, that
tactic failed dismally. Johnny and Danny were so
used to winning their own football that they had
no idea how to lock down an opponent. Not only
did the two opposition rovers continue to dom-
inate, but the Booyong pair wandered around
the ground looking totally lost, and they began
to lose confidence.

Paul Solomon was fighting a losing battle
in the back half and his frustration was beginning to get the better of him. Specky noticed it
first and brought it up with Mr Rutherford, just
minutes before the half-time siren.

'I think Sols needs a break,' he said. 'He gets
this look in his eyes and starts to lose focus a bit.

Maybe you should take him off now for a spell before he does something silly.'

Mr Rutherford agreed, but just as he sent the runner with that message, Sols charged at a Tigers' player kicking for goal. The ball missed, but Sols didn't, colliding with the player well after he had kicked. The umpire produced a yellow card and sent him to the sin bin for fifteen minutes.

Mercifully, the siren sounded and the Booyong players trudged to the change rooms, but not before the Tremont High player, who had been awarded another kick due to Sols' late bump, slotted through the opposition's eighth goal for the half.

The scoreboard read:

Tremont High Tigers	8	3	51
Booyong Lions	2	4	16

The margin was 35 points.

Mr Rutherford was bent over the whiteboard, switching players in an attempt to find a spark. The rest of the room was deadly quiet.

'C'mon, boys, lift your heads,' urged Specky, who couldn't help himself. 'We're not that bad and you all know it. Forget about the score – that doesn't matter right now.'

'Is that right? Who asked you?' interrupted Kyle.

'Kyle! How about you listen to what Simon has to say?' said Mr Rutherford before the other boys could react. 'You know Simon is helping me on the boundary line, so I guess you could say *I* asked him.'

Specky was surprised by Mr Rutherford's support, and the team looked pleased as Kyle pulled a face and crossed his arms angrily.

'Look, it's easy for me to say,' Specky continued, 'because I'm just standing on the boundary line, not doing anything. And I'm not trying to be a smart alec or anything. I just *know* we're a lot better than this. I've played with you guys for a long time now, and you've worked too hard to let this game slip away.'

Specky now had everyone's attention, including a large group of spectators who had crammed into the change rooms. All of a sudden, he began to feel self-conscious. But just as he thought it might be better if he shut up, Mr Rutherford interjected, sensing his uncertainty.

'Go on, Simon.'

Specky took a deep breath and continued. 'Look, I think maybe we've just got to get rid of all the negative thoughts you've got at the moment. I know that Johnny and Danny are just as good as Miller and DePaglia. Maybe we should just let Johnny and Danny play their own game.'

'Yeah, stick it to 'em, boys.' It was Robbo, who was beginning to follow Specky's train of thought.

'That's the way, Robbo,' encouraged Specky. 'Trust in each other, boys. Sols, we know you didn't mean to get sent off. Boys, that's just his way of trying a bit too hard. When you come back on, mate, everyone will support you one hundred percent.'

The room began to stir and the silence that was so heavy moments ago was replaced by encouraging talk from the rest of the team.

'C'mon, let's get back into this, one goal at a time,' said Michael Simpson, the Lions' determined back-pocket player.

'C'mon, Danny,' added Gobba. 'Show that DePaglia that there's only room for one Italian Stallion in this competition.'

'That's my boy!' came a voice from the crowd. 'You can-a do it, *figlio* . . . you bloody beauty!'

The whole room turned to see Danny's father, Antonio, standing on a bench, urging Danny on.

'Oh, brother!' said Danny, as he joined Robbo for their warm-up. 'There's nothing like an emotional Italian father to embarrass his son.'

'Don't worry about it.' Robbo grinned, slapping Danny on the back. 'He loves ya, mate. I reckon it's great.'

Mr Rutherford took up where Specky left off and, without raising his voice, urged the boys to just take it contest by contest. He set them the goal of reducing the lead to 15 points by three-quarter time. He took Specky's advice and released the shackles on Danny and Johnny, and he advised Sols that he would move him to centre-half forward the second his fifteen-minute penalty was up. Finally, he turned to Gobba, who was sitting quietly in the corner.

'Ben, I think we might need your special commentary to call us home, too, if it's all right by you.'

Gobba sprang to his feet with a new lease on life.

'Whatever you say, Mr Rutherford.'

Specky smiled at what was unfolding. The

Booyong Lions were not just going to lie down and die. And Mr Rutherford was starting to understand how they worked as a team – maybe he wasn't going to be such a bad coach after all. Specky did notice, however, that Mr Rutherford hadn't given his son any instructions. Despite the fact that Kyle had been less than friendly towards him since arriving at Booyong, Specky took a risk and made his way over to him.

Kyle looked at him warily, but Specky ignored it and, above the noise that was building in the rooms, he said, 'Kyle, I've played on that guy you're on a couple of times. He's strong, but he's slow. That's why he always plays five metres in front of you. Keep moving up to him and he'll keep moving forward. Eventually, you'll find that you have twenty-five metres of space behind you, and if you talk to Robbo, Danny and Johnny, and tell them to kick the ball long over his head, you'll kick some goals for sure.'

Kyle just shrugged and said, 'Whatever.'

Specky gave up and moved off to join the rest of the boys on the boundary.

The Booyong Lions played their hearts out in the second half. Danny and Johnny more than matched their opponents, Miller and DePaglia, and each of them managed to score a goal in the third quarter. Robbo continued to battle in the ruck. Michael Simpson and Gus Turner, the Lions' full-backs, continually denied the Tremont High forwards an opportunity to score goals, and Smashing Sols, having completed his time in the sin bin, tore back on to the ground and ran around like a kamikaze pilot. He played like a man possessed, laying crunching tackle after crunching tackle, his ferocious attack on the football inspiring his team-mates to even greater heights.

Booyong managed to cut the lead to 20 points by three-quarter time. Kyle kicked the first goal of the last quarter, courtesy of a long pass over the top of his opponent's head from Danny that made it possible for Kyle to run into an open goal. This narrowed the gap to 14 points.

Specky looked in Kyle's direction, wondering if he'd acknowledge him in any way, since it looked as if his half-time advice was paying off. Kyle didn't.

Gobba, who'd had a brief run in the third quarter, was back on the bench in full voice.

The crowd is going nuts here with just ten minutes to go in this epic Grand Final. Booyong, down and out at half-time, has somehow managed to dig deep and claw their way back into this game. Oh, how they would love to have Simon Magee out on the park at this very moment. If anyone could get the Lions home from here it would be him. But, having said that, folks, I can tell you every single player in this side has lifted in the second half and now this very, very good Tremont High team are looking a little vulnerable.

For the next ten minutes, it was the sort of football you would expect from a Grand Final. Both teams threw themselves into the action with no concern for their own welfare. It was a tough, bruising affair and, with rain beginning to fall, the mighty effort was beginning to take its toll.

Robbo was down with a bad cramp, Johnny was exhausted and barely able to lift his legs, and Danny, much to the horror of his family in the stands, had just been cleaned up fairly with a hip-and-shoulder on the outer wing.

Without Robbo to contest the boundary throw-in, the Tremont Tigers won the clearance and kicked the ball long into their forward line. Michael Simpson valiantly punched the ball clear of his opponent only to see it land straight in the arms of Ethan Miller, who straightened up and drilled the ball through the middle of the goals.

The Tremont supporters erupted. The margin was back to 20 points, and with just minutes to go they knew they were home.

The ball came back to the centre and Smashing Sols raised one last mighty effort, barrelling in off the square and gathering the ball. As he fed a hand-pass out to Danny, the siren sounded.

The Tremont Tigers had won.

The ecstatic Tremont supporters streamed on to the field, hugging and congratulating their players.

The Booyong players slumped to the ground, too exhausted and shattered to move.

18. raw nerve

Specky hopped off the tram, crossed Bridge Road, and made his way through the main entrance doors of the Epworth Hospital in Richmond. As he approached the information desk to find out which room his grandpa was in, he heard his name called out. Specky turned. It was his dad.

'You came straight from the gallery?' asked Specky, knowing that his father had been in at work to make up for the time he was spending at the hospital.

'Yeah. I'll probably have to be in there tomorrow as well, I'm afraid. Did Booyong win the Grand Final this morning?'

Specky sighed.

'Hmm. I guess that says it all. Look, Simon, I'm sorry you couldn't play, I really am . . .'

'Dad, it's cool. Really it is. How's Grandpa doing?'

'He's okay, considering. The doctor says he has to stay under observation for a while. He's on the third floor, room three five six. Go up if you like, I just want to finish my coffee. I'll join you soon.'

Specky made his way to the room and knocked quietly on the half-open door.

'I think you have a visitor, Mr Magee,' said a nurse taking Grandpa Ken's blood pressure.

Propped up in bed, Grandpa Ken's face lit up. Specky could see that he was thinner than he had been and it made him look much older. He was in his pyjamas and his arm was attached to a drip, but his smile was exactly the same.

'Here he is,' he said, happily. 'This is my grandson!'

'Oh, the football champion,' remarked the nurse, as she took the blood pressure strap off. 'I've heard all about you from your grandfather. Nice to meet you. My best friend's cousin is Nick Del Santo. Are you going to be as good as he is?'

'He's gonna be better than Nick Del Santo and Gary Ablett all rolled into one,' Grandpa Ken said proudly, before Specky could answer.

'Wow. That's a big call!' The nurse grinned. 'I'd better get your autograph now then.'

Specky blushed. Talk about embarrassing. Del Santo and Ablett were absolute legends of the game. If he turned out to be even a quarter as good as they were, he'd be happy.

'Well, I'll leave you two to catch up then.'

The nurse left the room and Specky pulled up a chair beside the bed. 'So, how're you doing?' he asked.

'I'm okay, for a sick old bugger,' said Grandpa Ken, 'but I'm still a little wobbly on my feet. Did your school team win? Tell me every detail.'

Specky described the game, play by play. Then he told Grandpa Ken about his injury.

'Well, I'm sorry to hear that, lad,' he said. 'But I agree. You have to be one hundred percent for your big game on the mighty MCG.'

'Yeah.' Specky smiled just thinking about it. 'I hope you'll be well enough to come and see me play.'

'Don't you worry about that. They'd have to

chain me up to stop me. I wouldn't miss it for quids. You never know what could come out of this game in terms of your future.'

'Well, Grub, our coach, said that some of us are in the running for the All-Australian side that will go to play in Ireland, which would be amazing . . .'

Specky didn't finish his sentence – Grandpa Ken had tears streaming down his cheeks and was quickly wiping them away.

'Are you okay?' asked Specky. What had he said to spark this emotional response?

'Yeah, yeah,' sniffed Grandpa Ken. 'Just this medication I'm on. Makes me bloody cry at the drop of a hat. Sorry, Simon. I'm proud of you, kid. You know that? And I hope you play the game of your life on Saturday. But, if you don't mind, I'm going to have a bit of a kip. Feeling a little tired. I'll see you later, okay?'

Specky nodded and left his grandpa to rest. While walking back to the lifts, he bumped into his dad in the corridor.

'You leaving already?' asked Mr Magee. 'How is he?'

'He wanted to have a nap,' said Specky.

'He seemed a bit upset when I mentioned the All-Australian side. Hey, Dad? You know how Grandpa was good at sport when he was younger? How good was he?'

Mr Magee's face hardened. Specky had obviously hit a raw nerve.

'Why? Did he say something? About me?'

'No! No! Why are you getting so defensive?' Specky blurted. 'It's crazy, Dad. I know he gets on your case a bit, but I don't understand why you two can't just get along.'

Mr Magee sighed heavily and gestured for Specky to sit down beside him on some nearby chairs. 'You're right,' he said. 'I am defensive. When it comes to your grandfather and me, I suppose that's the only way I know how to be. And I'm sorry if that's made things uncomfortable for you and Alice over the last few weeks. I'll try and explain, but I don't really know where to start.'

Specky looked at his father as if to say, well, go on.

'Look, there's no doubt that at one stage of my father's life, sport was his world. He lived for it, dare I say, the same way you live for footy. And, yes, to answer your question . . . yes, he was very good at it. All of it – football, tennis, but especially cricket. He was even selected for the Australian team.'

'He what? Are you serious?' said Specky, leaning forward. 'That's unreal! Why haven't you or Mum ever told me that?'

'Well, I don't really talk about my father at all, do I? I haven't really had much to do with him for the past ten years, remember?'

'Wow!' said Specky, still processing what his dad had told him. 'No wonder he was all emotional when I mentioned the All-Australian team. He played for Australia!'

'Well, no, he didn't play exactly,' said Mr Magee. 'His girlfriend, your grandma, fell pregnant around the same time he was selected. He had to work to support her and his child, so he gave up his position on the team –'

'Gave it up? No way!'

Mr Magee nodded sadly, and something dawned on Specky. 'That first child was you, right?'

'Yes,' said Mr Magee.

Specky paused, his mind hurriedly ticking over. 'But lots of sports stars have families.'

'Not in those days,' said Specky's dad. 'Sports

people didn't get paid the way they do today. He had to do the decent thing – marry his girl-friend, earn a living and support his family. It's been the biggest regret of his life. And I suppose that's why we don't get on.'

Again, Specky took a moment to process all that his father was telling him. 'You mean, he blames you?' he asked.

'Well, not directly, but I think he's always resented me. You know what I'm like at sport.'

'Yeah, you suck big-time, Dad,' stirred Specky, with a grin.

'Yeah, well, I know. And I'm glad you can see the humour in it because for my father it was deadly serious. My brother and I may not have inherited his sporting genes, but that wasn't going to stop him from desperately trying to mould us into mini-versions of him. He was per-sistent, that's for sure. There just came a point where I didn't want to deal with all of that – I didn't want to feel like a disappointment any-more. I wanted to create my own life.'

Mr Magee slumped back against the wall and crossed his arms. Specky felt for him. And for Grandpa Ken, too.

'You know what?' Specky said, determined to change things between them. 'I don't think Grandpa resents you. I think he loves you. Just think about it – he knew he didn't have long, but still he came here. He didn't tell you he was sick. He didn't want anything from you. He just wanted to spend his dying days with you. Maybe this was his way of saying, let's stop having a go at each other and get on with it? Maybe when you get a look at death head-on, the past isn't important anymore . . .'

Specky's father sat up and gave him a look. 'You're really impressing me right now, you know that?'

Specky smiled.

'Look, I can't promise anything, okay?' Mr Magee added. 'But you're absolutely right. Our stupid feuding isn't important anymore. Thanks to you!' Mr Magee hugged Specky, and made his way to see Grandpa Ken.

Specky watched him go and then walked towards the lifts, feeling pleased with himself. But before he got there, he heard his father shout for a nurse.

Within seconds, nurses and doctors were

rushing to Grandpa Ken's room. Specky ran back, only to be pushed aside as the medical staff hurriedly wheeled equipment into Grandpa Ken's room.

'Dad! What's going on?' Specky called to him.

'Just call your mother!' he shouted back, before closing the door on him.

19. throat tonic

Specky forced himself out the door on Monday morning and slowly shuffled his way to school.

His dad had come home from the hospital on Saturday night, devastated, and told them that Grandpa Ken had slipped into a coma. Their Sunday had been spent between the hospital and home – moping about aimlessly and praying he would come out of it.

'Hey, Speck, get a load of this.' Robbo waved him over as he entered the classroom. His mates were all gathered around Gobba. Mr Rutherford hadn't arrived for first period yet. 'Go on, Gob, say something,' Robbo ordered.

Gobba struggled to talk. Nothing came out but a hoarse whisper. He pointed to his throat.

'He's lost his voice,' said Danny.

At first Specky thought his friends were joking. And he was definitely in no mood that morning for jokes. 'Yeah, right. Well, at least his arm's healed up,' he said, turning to look for a place to sit.

'Are you okay?' asked TG, as she dropped her books on a table next to him. 'How's your grandpa?'

'Not good,' said Specky. 'Really bad, actually.' But before he could say more he was dragged back into his friends' conversation.

'Speck. We're serious!' said Danny.

'Mate, is this true?' Specky asked. He knew that the Cork in the Ocean commentary contest meant as much to Gobba as the National Final did to him.

Gobba nodded, looking miserable.

'But the game is at the end of this week. Will you be better by then?'

Gobba nodded, then he quickly scribbled something on a piece of paper and shoved it in front of Specky. It read, *I have laryngitis! The doctor said it's from overuse and I just have to rest my voice. I have to try not to talk for five whole days!*

Woah, thought Specky. That's a big ask. That's torture for someone like Gobba. At least it would be better in time for the contest.

While Specky had been talking to Gobba, Robbo and Johnny had been whispering and laughing together.

'Maybe Mrs Castellino can cook up a remedy,' suggested Robbo. 'Didn't she brew up something using, like, a ton of garlic when you were sick once, Danny? Or was that your aunty? Some old Sicilian brew, right?'

Danny didn't respond. Specky and the others saw him gazing across the room at the Gladiator. She was laughing and chatting with friends in the far corner of the classroom, oblivious to him staring at her.

'Oi! Stallion!' said Robbo, lightly punching him in the shoulder. 'I just asked you something.'

'What?'

'Don't worry about it, Saint Valentine,' Robbo said.

'If we had the eyes of a red tree frog, I could help ya,' remarked Johnny.

'Red tree frog eyes?' repeated Robbo. 'You're kidding?'

'Nah, it's my family's old Aboriginal remedy for sore throats,' Johnny explained. 'If he ate those beauties, he'd have his voice back in a couple of hours.'

Johnny winked at Specky. Robbo was having trouble keeping a grin off his face.

Gobba frantically mimed something to Johnny, his hands waving all over the place. It didn't take much to work out that he wanted to find out where you could find a red tree frog in Melbourne.

'Dunno,' shrugged Johnny. 'But I've heard blended spinach and beetroot juice do the same thing.'

Gobba was falling for it big-time.

'Yeah, I heard that, too!' said Robbo. 'My dad's mate is a race caller and whenever he starts to lose his voice he has a big glass of that. It's gross, but it works.'

Gobba winced at the thought of it.

He's not really going to drink that, is he? Specky thought. He must know they're having him on.

'Okay, Gob, at recess we're gonna ask the canteen ladies if they can help us out,' Robbo said.

'I reckon they'll blend some spinach and beet-root for ya and then –'

'ALL RIGHT! ENOUGH OF THE CHIT-CHAT! TIME FOR WORK!' bellowed Mr Rutherford, walking into the room. 'Just because this is your last week of term, doesn't mean you can slack off. Open your notebooks and scroll down to page forty-four of last week's file. I want you to take a good look at these problems because these are the kinds of questions you'll be working on during the holidays.'

Everyone groaned.

When recess finally rolled around, Specky's friends couldn't get to the back door of the canteen quickly enough. Specky, on the other hand, rushed to get in line at the front. He hadn't been in the mood to eat much at home and now he was starving.

'Grab me some chips, will ya?' said TG, jumping in line beside him. 'So, tell me, what's going on with your grandpa? Are you okay?'

Specky told her the sad news. He hadn't said

it out loud before and hadn't been able to bring himself to tell his mates. It felt good telling TG though. He found himself staring again into her green eyes. Could they be more than just friends? he wondered.

'Seriously? A coma? I'm sorry, Speck,' she said. 'Now I really understand the gloomy face you've had on all morning. Is there anything I can do?'

'Nah, but thanks. It's funny, you know, from the hospital you can almost see the MCG. I reckon Grandpa Ken would like that.'

'Yeah, and I bet he's liked being in Melbourne around Grand Final time. I was in the city on the weekend and you should have seen all the AFL decorations around. I love this time of the year. It's the best. Too bad the Tigers aren't in the Grand Final . . . but their day will come.'

'As long as you don't mind being in your eighties when it does,' teased Specky.

'Hey!' Tiger Girl grinned, and punched him in the arm. 'Oh, guess what – I'm still gonna see you play at the MCG. I thought there was no way Robbo would want me to come along after we broke up, but I gotta hand it to your mate, he's a good guy. I was so upset when I thought I'd miss your big game. He knew how much I was looking forward to it.'

It's now or never, thought Specky. I've got to say something. I've got to ask. 'Um, TG?' he said. 'Would you ever, um . . . would you ever consider . . .'

'What?' she asked.

'Nothing, it doesn't matter.'

'No, come on. What did you want to ask me? Would I ever consider what?'

'YO, SPECK! Come and check this out!'

Specky turned to see his friends gathering around Gobba as he prepared to drink down the disgusting homemade tonic of beetroot and spinach.

'Come on! Have a look at this,' yelled Robbo.

'Um . . .' Specky turned back to Tiger Girl.

'You boys are mental,' she said. 'Go! But will you ask me what you were going to ask me later?'

Specky nodded, before leaving his spot in the line and joining his friends.

'This is it, Gob,' said Danny, winding him up. 'Scull it in one gulp!'

Specky caught Gobba nervously glancing his

way as he raised the cup to his lips. Robbo gave him the thumbs-up.

Gobba swigged the 'tonic' in one go. He wiped the juice off his mouth with the back of his hand and burped. At first he looked okay, but within seconds his face turned an off-white colour and he was doubled over vomiting the sour concoction back up. A putrid red gush of liquid hit the quadrangle, splattering for almost a metre in all directions. Some nearby Year Seven girls squealed, and Specky's friends started laughing, including Gobba, who had juice dribbling out his nose.

'What is going on here?' growled Mr Rutherford, appearing out of nowhere. 'You boys, clean this up at once! Higgins, if you're sick, go and see the school nurse. Magee, come here, please.' Mr Rutherford stormed off.

Why's he singling me out now? thought Specky. 'I didn't do anything,' he called.

'Now, Magee!'

20. another blessing

'Simon, can you duck out and get some milk, please?' asked Mrs Magee, popping her head into Specky's bedroom. 'We don't have much to offer Mr Rutherford when he gets here, so get some Tim Tams or something as well. Are you sure you don't know why he's coming to see us? Are you sure it isn't about you being in more trouble? It's very bad timing in light of what's happened with Grandpa Ken, but I'm sure he understands that.'

'Yeah, but he said he only wants to talk to you briefly. I haven't done anything, Mum – promise. He just said he wanted to talk to you about something personal.'

'Well, here,' added Specky's mother, handing

him some money. 'And put a jumper on. It's cold outside.'

Specky walked in the chilly night air to the local milkbar. It was only a couple of streets away from his house. On his way back, he became aware of car headlights behind him on the dark quiet street and it seemed as if they were keeping pace with him. He quickened his stride a little and, sure enough, the car increased its speed as well.

Yep, it's definitely following me, thought Specky, his heart now thumping. Maybe it's that mysterious bald man from the airport and from State training? he thought. Or that creepy talent manager, Brad Dobson. But why would he be following me like this? Maybe he's not a manager at all, but some crazed stalker . . . Yeah, some crazed stalker who probably has a huge knife, or worse . . . a chainsaw? Specky's mind was racing and before he knew it he was jogging, then running – which was surprisingly difficult to do carrying a carton of milk and a pack of Tim Tams. When he reached the front door of his house, Specky turned to see the mysterious car actually pulling up into his driveway.

'What the?' Specky gasped, trying to catch his breath. 'What's he going to do? Kill me on my doorstep?'

Just as Specky was about to open the front door and bolt inside, Mr Rutherford hopped out of the car.

'I thought that was you,' he said, smiling and striding across the lawn. 'Wasn't sure if I was in the right street. Good to see you getting a run in – keeping fit before the big game.'

Specky laughed with relief as he led Mr Rutherford into the house and introduced him to his parents.

'Thanks again for your time,' Mr Rutherford began, 'especially considering what you're going through with your father. I hope he gets well soon.'

'Thank you,' said Mr Magee. 'So, um, what can we do for you, John? Why the urgency to see us in person?'

'Well, I'm actually here to apologise to Simon. And I felt it should be done in your presence. I regret that there's been a terrible mix-up with the Maths test Simon took. The test I thought was his, I discovered later, was not,' he explained.

'Yes!' Specky said. 'I told you!'

'Simon, please,' said Mrs Magee. 'What do you mean it wasn't his test?'

Mr Rutherford took a deep breath. Specky could hardly contain himself.

'Well, when Simon said it wasn't his handwriting on the test, I brushed it off as a desperate excuse. But the other day my wife found Simon's real test in my son's bedroom. Apparently, my son, Kyle, had exchanged it with a test he had filled in himself, with most of the questions answered incorrectly.'

'That dirty rotten little –'

'Simon!' snapped Specky's mother.

'No, it's okay, Mrs Magee. Simon has every right to be angry,' said Mr Rutherford. 'What Kyle did is unforgivable.'

'Why would your son do this?' asked Specky's dad.

'That's not an easy question to answer. I think, on some level, Kyle feels threatened by Simon. At his last school, Kyle was a big fish in a small pond in terms of his footy skills and status. He loved his mates and they loved him. I've come to see he deeply resented having to leave. So even though he took his frustrations out on Simon, I think his actions were really aimed at me. It's not easy for children of teachers to attend the same school – there's always a certain added pressure for them to do well. I know Kyle has felt that pressure and we've moved twice in four years because of my career. But having said that, we've always struggled to get along. We've never really . . . um . . . what's the word I'm looking for?'

'Clicked?' said Specky.

'Yes, clicked, exactly.' Mr Rutherford nodded. 'I know it may sound strange for a father and son not to click, but –'

'Not that strange,' said Mr Magee, shooting a forlorn look at Mrs Magee.

'Yes, well, that's the way it is with Kyle and me at the moment,' continued Mr Rutherford. 'I'm sorry that our problems have affected you, too. Simon, I hope you can understand how upset I am that you missed the game. You worked hard to pass that second test and you should have been rewarded for that.'

'Um, Dad?' Alice popped her head around the door. 'That's the hospital on the phone. They want to talk to you. It sounds urgent.'

'Excuse me, John,' said Specky's dad, standing up. 'I've got to take this.' Mr Magee hurriedly left the room.

'Well, I think I've taken up enough of your time,' Mr Rutherford said, standing up to shake Mrs Magee's hand.

'So, does that mean I did pass?' asked Simon.

'Sorry?' said Mr Rutherford.

'Did I pass the test?'

'Yes, you did,' smiled Mr Rutherford. 'In fact, you did exceptionally well. You scored forty-four out of fifty. Of course, it would've been forty-six if I hadn't take those two marks off.'

Specky beamed, as did his mum. It was really nice to get some good news in what had been a long few days of gloom.

Specky showed Mr Rutherford out.

'Simon, I'll see you next term. Have a good break,' he said sincerely. 'And all the best this weekend for the National Final. I know I've been tough on you, but you're a real talent – and that means you need to be challenged. I hope you understand that. I just expect a lot from you because I think you can live up to those expectations.'

'Thanks, Mr Rutherford,' said Specky, who now looked at his Maths teacher differently. 'I'll do my best.'

As he closed the door behind his teacher, Specky realised that he was very much looking forward to playing football under Mr Rutherford. He was starting to understand that there was no right or wrong formula that determined whether a coach was successful or not. He ran through a mental list of the current AFL coaches and quickly found that they all went about their jobs differently. He thought of Paul Roos, the coach of Sydney – a famously relaxed coach, who rarely lost his temper, and was the only senior coach who regularly coached from the boundary line rather than the coaches box. Both of these things set him apart from the other fifteen coaches, but neither of them stopped him from coaching the Swans to a Premiership. In a similar style, Coach Pate was really positive in everything she said. Rather than dwell on the mistakes that her players made she was more inclined to highlight those things they did well. But Mr Rutherford was more demanding of his players – on the ground and off. Specky's State coach, Grub Gordan, was an extremely hard task master, too, but Specky had been prepared for this as his reputation preceded him. He realised now that he had resented Mr Rutherford because he wasn't the sort of coach that he thought he would be – rather than treat each coach on their merits, he had already made up his mind as to how Mr Rutherford should go about the role.

Still thinking about coaches, Specky nearly ran into his dad, who was stomping down the stairs with his car keys jiggling in his hands.

'What's going on?' Specky asked.

'Your grandfather is waking up,' he said, smiling. 'The old bugger is coming to!'

21. national final

The alarm clock went off at six-thirty on the morning of the National Final, but Specky had been tossing and turning all night and was already awake. It had been an emotional week, to say the least. The news that Grandpa Ken was awake and resting comfortably had lifted his spirits immensely. After two full-on training sessions with the team earlier in the week, the day he'd been waiting for had finally arrived.

'This is it,' Specky said to himself as he jumped out of bed. He ran through a quick couple of stretching exercises and to his great relief didn't feel one bit of tightness in his buttock or down his hamstring.

'Be at the ground by eight am, team meeting

at eight-ten, warm-up on the ground at nine-ten, and the game starts at nine-thirty.'

Specky had repeated this to himself a thousand times over the last week. And what a whirlwind the last few days had been. His mobile phone had not stopped ringing. It seemed every person he had ever met wanted to wish him well for the big game. It was great to know he had so much support, but at eight o'clock the night before he'd had no other choice but to turn his phone off. He just wanted to watch a movie, try and get his mind off the game for a bit, and get a couple of hours sleep.

Specky knew that schedules played a big part in the daily lives of AFL players and that they were expected to be on time for everything. Because the AFL Grand Final was one of the biggest sporting events in the country and the pre-game entertainment was a massive part of the day, the Under-Fifteen National Final was scheduled to start very early. Specky had gone over the timetable sent to him by Bobby Stockdale a hundred times. The very last thing he wanted was to be caught in traffic and arrive late to the biggest game of his young sporting life.

Specky had a shower, methodically packed his bag – making sure five times that he wasn't forgetting anything – and then made his way to the kitchen, his mind totally on the game. When he looked up, he got the surprise of his life. Standing behind the kitchen table was his whole family, and Danny and Robbo. They were all grinning from ear to ear – except for Jack, who was gurgling.

'Wha . . . what? What are you guys doing?' Specky managed to get out. 'It's six-thirty in the morning!'

'Well, O Chosen One,' said Alice. 'Even I know how big a day this is for you, and we all wanted to let you know how very proud we are. My little brother, about to play at the MCG – who would've thunk it?'

'Yeah, Speck, even Robbo and I haven't been able to sleep for a couple of days,' said Danny. 'It's almost as if we're playing, too. Your mum asked us over for breakfast, just to help ya settle the nerves and stuff.'

'You'll kill 'em today, Speck,' added Robbo. 'You've been ready for this game since the day you were born.'

'Right,' said Mrs Magee. 'I've got some mouths to feed.'

It was only then that Specky noticed what was on the kitchen table. It looked like a buffet on a cruise ship or a health resort. There were bottles of Gatorade and water, platters of fruit, mountains of pancakes, bowls of hot spaghetti and baked beans, and wobbly stacks of multigrain toast.

Specky grinned. 'Umm, Mum, you've done an awesome job, but there's enough here to feed the whole team. Grub told us to try and keep to our normal pre-game routine, so I'll probably only have some spaghetti on toast, and take a couple of bananas for the trip.'

'Well, that's okay, love – I just wanted to make sure. You've trained me so well over the past eighteen months, I think I could get a job with a real club as their dietician.'

'Don't worry, Mrs M,' said Robbo as he speared a stack of pancakes and drowned them in maple syrup. 'Danny and I will help you out.'

For the first time in what seemed like weeks, Specky was able to forget about the game for a few moments as he and his friends gulped down their breakfast.

'Okay, then,' interrupted Mr Magee, as he grabbed his car keys and handed Jack to Alice. 'We better get you to the ground, Simon. Can't have you being late.'

'Are you and Grandpa going to watch me on the telly?'

'Yep. We're going to watch it together live from his room. I think he's told every nurse and doctor in the hospital about it. This will be a big day for us, too. If you know what I mean.'

Specky smiled. He was thrilled that football was finally bringing Grandpa Ken and his dad together, instead of driving them apart – but he couldn't think about it too much as the nerves were beginning to kick in.

Specky and his dad pulled into the drop-off bay outside the MCG. Specky retrieved his bag from the boot of the car and waved his father goodbye as he drove off to the hospital.

Specky looked up at the magnificent MCG. His spine tingled. Marquees and food stalls surrounded the ground and massive flags promoting the AFL Grand Final were fluttering high above the stadium. The city of Melbourne was talking about nothing else. For as long as Specky could remember, this had always been the most exciting day of the year. There'd been a buzz building around town all week and now the day had finally arrived – and he was going to be a part of it!

Specky could scarcely believe it. He was one of the privileged few who were going to play on this hallowed surface today. His legs began to feel like jelly.

Since it was still early, there weren't many people at the gate when he presented his ticket. Once inside, he took the lift down to the change rooms. There were television trucks parked under the ground with kilometres of cable winding their way up into the stands, hundreds of catering people preparing the tons of food that would be consumed that day, and thousands of kids rehearsing their routines for the pre-game show.

When Specky reached the Victorian team's change rooms, Bobby Stockdale was at the door marking off names.

'Good to see you, Simon. Big day ahead, son. You wouldn't want to be anywhere else.'

Specky moved into the rooms in a daze. They were strangely familiar. He had seen them hundreds of times in television footage of players warming up before a game or celebrating after a victory.

These are the same rooms that Judd, Brown, Fevola, Ablett, Hodge, McLeod, Kirk, Pavlich, Cornes and Riewoldt all get changed in, Specky thought to himself as he put his bag at the foot of a locker.

A huge smile came over his face and, strangely, all the nervous sensations he had been feeling completely disappeared. Specky had never felt more comfortable than he did right now.

'This is where I want to be,' he whispered.

The biggest and most important football game of his life was about to begin.

Grub Gordan stood in front of a massive covered whiteboard in the cavernous meeting room. Specky sat in front of him, thrilled to be one of the twenty-two best Under-Fifteen footballers in Victoria and proud to be wearing the big white V on his navy blue jumper.

'You wear this jumper for a reason,' Grub bellowed, before dramatically dropping the tone of his voice. 'Victorian football teams have the proudest reputation of any State team in this country. We respect our opposition and their right to be in this final, but we EXPECT to win every time a team wearing that big V jumper takes the field. It doesn't matter if it's the bloody Victorian kindergarten team or the Victorian AFL team.'

Specky and his team-mates had been shown a motivational DVD about the history of Victorian football at the team meeting earlier in the week. The late great Ted Whitten had lived for the Big V, and his passion for the jumper was an inspiration for Specky and all his team-mates.

Grub reiterated this message before unveiling the team positions on the whiteboard. Specky searched for his name on the forward line, and, unable to see it, resigned himself to the fact that he would be starting on the bench.

After going through various instructions – and being constantly interrupted by an out-of-control

Dicky Atkins, who was almost frothing at the mouth in anticipation of the game – Grub turned and looked Specky in the eye.

'Simon, massive job for you today. We know that the South Australians have done their homework on our side. You are the equal leading goal scorer for the whole carnival so they will be expecting you to line up in the forward line. Ever heard of Matthew Richardson?'

Specky nodded. Was he serious? Who hadn't heard of Richo? The champion Richmond veteran had had a blinder season at the age of 33, when he finished equal third in the Brownlow Medal, just two votes behind the winner, Adam Cooney.

'That's the role we want you to play today. Richo was moved to the wing that year and allowed to run all over the ground. He's a magnificent athlete, with great endurance, so he was able to take saving marks in defence one minute and kick goals in the forward line the next. We know you can do the same thing.'

Specky nodded his head again, recalling some of the great games he had watched Richo play throughout that year.

'You can do it, Speck,' bellowed Dicky, who was up on his feet, roaring at the top of his lungs.

'Settle down, Dicky,' said Grub, trying to get his big full-back to keep a lid on it for another couple of minutes. 'Boys, I want you to play through Magee out on his wing. There's plenty of room out there for him and I don't think they'll be able to match him in the air or on the ground.'

Specky just sat there taking it all in. He'd been compared to Matthew Richardson and learnt that one of the keys to their whole game plan had been built around him – what a morning! He was not going to let them down.

Grub finished his pre-game speech and the boys stormed out of the rooms. Specky went for a last-minute toilet break. He had drunk so much Gatorade to stay hydrated that he had already gone several times that morning. As he was washing his hands, Dicky rushed past him, just making it to the basin before heaving what seemed like three bottles of orange liquid into the basin.

'Sorry, Speck,' Dicky grinned, wiping his face. 'Happens all the time before a big game. I'm ready to go now, champ. Let's get out there and kick some butt.'

They made their way up the race towards the ground. Words of encouragement were flying between his team-mates and the sense of anticipation was like nothing Specky had ever experienced. He felt as if he could take on the world. He was pumped and knew what he had to do.

As the team entered the ground, Specky noticed a group of boys making their way around the boundary line towards the commentary box. It was Gobba and the three other commentary finalists. Specky pointed to his throat and gave him the thumbs-up, hoping Gobba's voice was fully recovered. Gobba just waved as he was escorted away.

Before Specky knew it, the Vics were running through the banner. The relatively small crowd that was there for the early game made a surprisingly loud noise. The grass on the ground was like carpet. There was not a breath of wind in the air and the sun was shining.

It was a perfect day for footy.

The Fox Sports commentary team of Brian

Paylor and Jim Bradshaw were in place, building the atmosphere magnificently as the umpire held the ball aloft to start the game.

Here we go, folks. The umpire's about to get this game underway. It's going to be a beauty, Jim.

Sure is, Brian. Grub Gordan has sprung the first surprise. We've been looking forward to watching this kid Magee kick goals for a couple of weeks, but he's starting on the wing. Let's watch that one closely.

The ball was bounced and the Vics' ruckman, 'Lurch' Freeman, got the first tap out. Specky had started on the members' side wing and he charged into the middle of the ground. Brian Edwards scooped the ball up and shot a handball out to Lenny 'Skull' Morgan, the Victorian rover. Specky quickly turned, leaving his opponent standing still, and moved back out towards the wing.

Morgan's got it for the Vics. You can't miss him, Jim, his bald cranium is as shiny as a bowling ball.

He's got some pace, too, Brian. Look out, he's about to get run down, but not before he shoots a handball out in front of Magee, into the wide spaces of the MCG. Look at this boy go, Brian.

Specky felt as if he were floating. He hadn't played for two weeks. His body was well rested and he felt unbelievable. He moved quickly towards the ball as it dribbled awkwardly away from him. Then he noticed a massive South Australian defender leaving his man and charging towards the bouncing ball. He had a flashback to his last game for Booyong.

'Not this time,' Specky said to himself as he set his eyes on the ball and nothing else.

Magee bends to pick up the ball, and – oh no, he's going to get cleaned up here, Brian.

Specky gathered the ball cleanly and as his opponent dropped his shoulder, looking to bump him off his feet, Specky turned his body sharply, executing a perfect blind turn. He found himself in clear space just outside the fifty-metre line.

Unbelievable! Magee somehow survives and now runs to the fifty-metre line. He looks inside, but all of the Victorian players have been manned up. He settles himself, gets balanced, and from forty metres out lines up the goals . . .

Specky took a deep breath. He could hear his team-mate Michael Bayless tell him he was clear so all he had to do was concentrate on the kick. He had looked to centre the ball, but the South Australians had a spare man in the hole so there was no free target. He dropped the ball on to his boot, aiming just inside the right goal post.

Magee kicks for goal. It looks okay . . . it's there! It's there! The Vics have got the first goal on the board inside thirty seconds. What an effort from young Simon Magee . . . Oh boy, what a start!

Specky's team-mates went wild. They ran to him from all around the ground, patting him on the back and ruffling his hair. Dicky Atkins had sprinted all the way from full-back, whooping and hollering the whole way like a banshee. 'You little beauty, Speck. Inspirational, champ!' He hugged him so hard, Specky thought his ribs were going to break. Brian Edwards gave him a high-five as he ran back to the middle of the ground.

He's something special, Jim, I'm telling you now. The South Australians are going to have to watch him carefully.

Specky took up his position on the wing for the next centre bounce when . . . *thwack*, he was bumped off his feet and found himself sprawled on the ground.

Oh, it's on here, Brian. Kevin Kottersly, the South Australian skipper, has sat Magee on his backside . . . Oh, look out, Malopolous for the Vics is in there, so is Hayes from South Australia. The young boys are letting off a bit of steam.

They are, Jim, but it's all pretty harmless. No punches thrown, just a bit of pushing and shoving. I think the South Aussie captain, Kottersly, just wanted to let Magee know that they weren't going to let him run around all day doing whatever he wants. Anyway, the umpire's done the right thing here and bounced the ball to resume play. That's the best way to stop any dust-up.

Specky picked himself up and ignored what was going on around him. The ball was kicked into the South Australian forward line, only to have big Dicky Atkins come barrelling out from full-back, gather the ball and steamroll right over the top of two opponents, swatting them away like flies.

Specky looked up the field and saw Lurch Freeman running into space. He sprinted towards him as Dicky sent a beautiful pass in his direction. Lurch marked it and fed off a hand-pass to Specky as he sprinted past. He tucked the ball under his arm, ran for ten metres, took a bounce, and then looked up the field. Trent Norris, the boy who had been named at full-forward for the Vics, pushed off his opponent and led beautifully up the middle of the ground.

Specky sent a sizzling pass that travelled thirty-five metres, right onto the chest of Norris, who took the mark in his hands, not giving the South Australian full-back a chance to spoil.

 The Vics are on fire here – Edwards and young Magee are right in the middle of the action. Norris goes back and drills through their second, and they're off to a flyer.

★ ★ ★

The half-time siren sounded with Victoria holding on to a seven-point lead. They made their way in to the rooms, encouraging each other the whole way off the ground. The game had turned into a terrific spectacle with the skills of both sides well and truly on display. Specky had sat the last five minutes on the bench – Grub had thought that he needed a rest.

From the bench Specky had glanced up into the stands, just to see if his family and friends were watching. He had looked on the internet the night before and knew where their seats were.

He could see his mum, Jack, Alice, the Great McCarthy, Robbo and, best of all, Tiger Girl.

Grub delivered a stirring half-time speech and to Specky's surprise even singled him out for his great attack on the ball in the first quarter. Specky was playing a great game, and despite the extra attention he was getting from the opposition, he was one of the reasons the Vics held a slender lead.

'One of the things we're getting caught out on is they're kicking in after we score a point,' Grub continued. 'Too many times we've allowed the ball to spill over the back of the pack and then they run it all the way into their forward line. I want the ball punched back – hard – from their kick-ins. Gleeson, Edwards and Morgan, you small blokes, get to the front of these packs and be first at the crumb.'

Grub made a few positional moves, including placing Specky back onto the wing.

'This is the quarter that can break this game open,' he roared as the Vics headed back out to the race.

Specky knew that this was also the quarter that Gobba would be calling for the Cork in the Ocean contest. As he ran on, he imagined him way up in the commentary box, positioning his headset – filled with nerves – sitting in a box next to two of his heroes, Jim Bradshaw and Brian Paylor. He knew that as long as Gobba's voice held out he would absolutely nail it.

★　★　★

The competition organiser pointed to Gobba as the red 'on air' button came to life in front of him.

'Welcome back to the MC . . . ahummph, MCG . . .'

Gobba froze. He hadn't talked all day for fear of not being able to call the game and now it looked as if those fears might have been well-founded. Everyone was looking at him, the organiser frantically indicating for him to go on.

'Ahummph, excuse me, folks,' Gobba managed. 'Sorry about that, a little frog in the throat.'

 What a rip-snorter we've got here today, folks. Two great young teams filled with the prodigious

talent that will carry this great game of ours for-
ward in the coming decade. Remember the names of
some of these lads and mark them down in your footy
records – for the Atkins, Morgans, Molopolouses and
Freemans of today will be the AFL stars of tomorrow.
And I get the feeling that the name Magee will be in
that group, too.

Everyone in the box looked on in awe as Gobba
moved into top gear, getting better as the game
progressed.

Five minutes to go in the third quarter and the
ball has been locked deep in the South Australian for-
ward line for what seems like an eternity. It spills out
to Johnson from South Australia, who flicks it over to
Hawley. He ducks one way . . . then another . . . then
throws it onto his boot. But Magee – Simon Magee –
flings himself, with no regard for his own safety,
onto the ball and smothers it. It comes free towards
Kottersly, the skipper for the crow-eaters, who shrugs
a tackle and heads towards goal. He baulks around
Bayless, spins past Edwards, and lines up the goals,
and . . . WOW WEE! What a bone-crunching tackle!

Who was that? I don't believe it. Magee has picked himself up after smothering the ball, only to lay an unbelievable tackle. I think Magee might have owed Kottersly one from earlier in the day.

After his mighty smother and tackle, Specky again found himself on the bench for the final minutes of the quarter. South Australia were playing the game of their lives and it was taking some inspirational football from the Vics just to stay ahead. Specky felt as if his lungs were bursting and his legs were burning.

 There goes the siren for the end of the third quarter, folks, and the Vics have managed to hang on to a tiny three-point lead. It's set up for a mighty final term. And that's it from me, but before I go I've got to say to my mates at Booyong High: Boys, the tonic worked beautifully. My voice has never sounded better.

★ ★ ★

After Grub finished addressing his players, Dicky Atkins took it upon himself to get the group together for one last rev-up before the final quarter.

Specky was heading towards the group, when Grub grabbed him by the arm and took him to one side.

Oh no! What have I done? thought Specky. Grub only ever spoke to a player one-on-one to point out something he had done wrong.

'Yes, Grub,' said Specky, looking his coach in the eye and expecting the worst.

'How ya feeling?' said Grub, his face giving nothing away.

'I'm good. I feel really good.'

'Not too tired?'

'Nah, I got a rub at three-quarter time and that spell on the bench helped,' said Specky.

'Excellent,' Grub replied, the hint of a smile on his face. 'Have a look around, Simon. I don't want you to forget this moment. You've worked your backside off for us in the first three quarters. Now, this is what it's all about. The great players step up on the big stage. There are about eighty-thousand people here now, probably closer to one hundred by the end of the game. I know I've been driving you hard, and I don't give out too much praise, but you've been great, son. Now go and finish it off.'

Specky felt an amazing surge of pride. He'd had to develop a thick skin with Grub over the months they'd trained together, and he'd copped more than his fair share of criticism along the way. But listening to Grub say those words made it all worthwhile.

Back on the field, waiting for the umpire to start the last quarter and watching the stands filling to capacity, Specky knew, right then, that he would do whatever it took to experience this feeling again at AFL level.

The Fox Sports commentary team got things going in the last quarter.

Can the Vics hold on, Brian? They looked tired in the last few minutes of that third quarter.

I'm sure they can, Jim. This crowd, which has built to about eighty-five thousand, will start roaring for them in this last quarter and I'm not sure that there will be too much support for the young boys from South Australia – given that we've got two Victorian teams set to battle it out in the main game in a couple of hours time.

But Specky wasn't so sure. He had never worked harder in his life. One minute he was floating in front of a pack taking marks in defense, and the next minute he was delivering the ball deep into his own forward line. Bear Gleeson and Brian Edwards had also run themselves into the ground and had played fantastically the entire game – but they were all simply running out of legs.

The wide-open spaces of the MCG were starting to take their toll. The South Australians had managed to kick three quick goals through Kottersly, who was absolutely on fire, and two goals went to their blond, high flying forward, Terry Backley. The Vics now trailed by 14 points and the game was slipping away.

'Grub wants you to go to centre-half forward, Speck. We need a couple of goals!'

Specky was so exhausted that he could barely acknowledge the runner. He managed to nod his head and ran to his position. The ball remained in the South Australian forward line for a couple of minutes, giving Specky a chance to catch his breath. But it also meant valuable time was ticking by.

Dicky Atkins retrieved the ball from the crowd after another behind by South Australia. As always, he had given his all. At the start of the quarter he had split his head open and been taken from the field due to the blood rule and down to the rooms to be stitched up. He had returned to the ground with a giant white bandage around his head. Specky thought he looked more fearsome than ever.

With time running out, Dicky barrelled a massive torpedo straight down the middle of the ground. The footy spiralled at least sixty metres, and the crowd roared its approval. Lurch Freeman tried to mark it, but it was punched to the ground before he could get his hands on it. Thankfully, Skull Morgan was waiting.

The ball's been punched forward and Morgan gathers it cleanly and shoots out a handball to Bayless. With the clock ticking down, Bayless swings onto his left foot in the direction of centre-half forward, but – oh no! – the South Australian ruckman, Harry Zatsaris,

has positioned himself there perfectly. But, wait . . .
MAAAAGGGEEEEEE! Simon Magee has come from
nowhere and perched himself on top of the shoulders of
Zatsaris to take one of the greatest marks you're ever
likely to see. Have a listen to this crowd, Jim.

Specky flipped himself forward after taking the
ball in his hands, completing a somersault in the
process. Almost landing on his head, he hit the
ground with a thud.

The thunderous cheer from eighty thousand
spectators echoed in Specky's ears. He tried to
compose himself as he went back to take his kick
for goal. With the team trailing by 15 points,
Specky knew he had to slot this one through to
give the Vics any sort of a chance.

So tired that he was almost acting on instinct,
Specky moved forward, guiding the ball to his
boot. From forty-five metres out, the footy sailed
straight through the middle of the goals, never
deviating.

Again, the crowd went berserk. The cheer
squads for the teams competing in the senior
AFL Grand Final were leading the chant for the
Victorians.

Magee holds the key, Jim. They've just got to give him the chance. What a game he's played. Back in the centre, Zatsaris wins the tap, but it's sharked by Edwards. Not mucking around, he bombs the ball long into the Vics forward line where Norris takes the tumbling mark. He's got it, Jim! The Vics are not finished yet. He lines it up. It looks good, but . . . no, it just drifts off-line. South Australia leads by eight – a minute and a half to go.

Specky took up his position in the zone. He knew there was not much time left.

He's taking his time, this South Australian full-back. He goes back and boots the ball long, towards the boundary line. Not a smart move, Brian – it's in the direction of Magee.

All the players were just about out on their feet, which allowed Specky to get a clear run at the ball. Both Lurch Freeman and Harry Zatsaris positioned themselves under it, ready to compete for the mark. With one last, mighty effort,

Specky launched himself at the ball again, getting a perfect ride on the backs of both ruckmen.

 Here comes MAAAGGEEEEE!

Specky was in perfect position, propped up on the shoulders of the ruckmen, but at the last moment, instead of attempting the mark, he punched the ball forward with all his might. With Grub's half-time instructions burning in his mind, Brian Edwards had perfectly read what Specky was going to do and ran in and masterfully crumbed the ball. He shot out a quick handball to Bear Gleeson, who ran into goal and put it straight through the big sticks. The MCG erupted.

 The Vics are coming! The Vics are coming!

Is there time, Brian? That's the only question. Gee, I thought Magee was going to take another specky, but he did the disciplined thing and his team-mates benefitted. What a game!

Specky stood at the front of the centre square and looked around him. All the South Australian players had moved into their own back line, determined to hang on to their two-point lead.

I don't know how much time's left, Jim, but this is the most crucial centre bounce of the day. The ball goes up and Zatsaris thumps it forward for the South Australians, but there's no one there. Except, DICKY ATKINS! He gathers the ball and looks up field . . .

BARRRRRRRGGGGHHHHHHH.

Siren, Jim! There goes the siren! South Australia have held on. They are the Under-Fifteen National Champions. This has been the ultimate battle of the young guns! Sensational! What a cracker of a game! If the senior Grand Final lives up to what we've just witnessed, we're in for a special day.

The South Australians went absolutely wild. Specky just stood there – numb, too tired and disappointed to move, acutely aware of the pain of having lost such a big game. As the ground staff quickly set up the stage for the presentation of the Cup, Grub Gordan waddled on to the ground and went over to shake the hands of the South Australian boys and their coach. Then he made his way over to the Vics.

'Come on, get up, ya lazy buggers,' he said, with a resigned smile on his face. 'I don't want any of you boys to walk off this ground disappointed. This is what football is all about. You tried your hearts out, right up to the very last second, and the siren happened to go at the wrong time. You're winners, boys, believe me.'

The team watched the South Australian coach and captain walk onto the stage to receive the Championship Cup. As they got off the dais, Specky started to head towards the change rooms, not really paying much attention to what was going on around him.

And the winner of the Robert Harvey medal for best player on the ground is . . . Simon Magee.

Specky stopped in his tracks, dumbfounded. Rarely did a player from the losing side win the best-on-ground award, and it hadn't once occurred to him that it might be him. A massive cheer came from the Victorian camp. For the first time since the siren sounded, his teammates managed to smile.

As he made his way towards the stage, the giant scoreboards at the MCG came to life. Looking up, Specky nearly fell over as he saw an image of himself soaring towards the clouds and taking a mark that would be spoken about for years to come.

He looked out at the crowd in the direction of his friends and family. For a split second, he thought he could see them jumping up from their seats. The roar from the crowd, as they all turned their attention to the big screens, was to rival any that came from the MCG on Grand Final day.

But that still wasn't the best thing that happened that day. That was still to come . . .

22. the unexpected

Specky opened the door to the hospital room and was surprised to find his dad and his grandpa chatting to each other as if they were old buddies.

'Here he is,' said Mr Magee proudly, getting out of his chair and wrapping his arms around Specky. 'I'm so proud of you!'

Specky hugged him back and then walked over to hug his grandpa. 'How are you?' he asked.

'I couldn't be better, kid! I was hoping you'd play well, but instead you played a blinder. My grandson is a champion.'

'So, you saw it?'

'Of course we saw it!' said Grandpa Ken. 'I know I promised to come and see you play, but

I got to do the next best thing – I saw you on the TV.'

'We watched every minute of it, Si,' added Specky's dad. 'And some of the nurses joined us – we had quite a crowd.'

'We had a beaut time, your father and me,' Grandpa said.

'You did? Really?' said Specky. 'I mean, you're not just saying that for me . . .'

'No, Simon, we're not,' said Mr Magee. 'Dad and I had a great time. We realised we have something very much in common – you. And we've decided that's a great place for us to make a fresh start. Now I'm going to leave you two to chat for a bit – I believe you have something to show your Grandpa, Si? Are the others here?'

'They're all in the canteen. Mum said that I should come up here on my own first and they would visit later.'

'Smart woman, my wife.' Mr Magee smiled. 'We'll see you in a few minutes.'

'So, let's have a closer look at that Robert Harvey medal of yours,' said Grandpa Ken.

Specky took the medal from around his neck and handed it to his grandpa.

'Brilliant. Just fantastic,' he mumbled.

'But I wanted to show you something else,' said Specky, opening a plastic bag he had carried in. 'I thought you might want to hold onto it for me until I use it.'

'What is it? A footy jumper?' Grandpa Ken asked as he turned it over to see the colours.

'Not just any jumper. It's an All-Australian jumper. After today's match our coach announced the All-Australian team – and I'm on it. We're touring Ireland in the International Rules Series.'

Grandpa Ken squeezed the jumper close to his chest – he seemed overcome with emotion. He didn't say a word.

'Are you okay?' Specky asked softly, noticing that he had tears in his eyes. 'Is it the medication again?'

'Nah, kid,' he sniffed. 'This is all me. All me. Thank you.'

Later that night, Danny, Robbo and Gobba appeared at the Magee's front door.

'Woo-hoo! Here he is! The best man on the ground!'

'You were awesome, man!'

'Unbelievable! Best footy ever!'

Specky beamed as his friends enthusiastically congratulated him. 'Thanks, guys,' he sighed. 'Talk about a full-on day, huh?'

'Speck, you were sensational – truly,' gushed Danny. 'Your game was even better than the actual Grand Final, especially the way that . . .'

Beep! Beep!

Danny reached into his pocket to check his mobile.

'Here we go again,' said Robbo. 'The Gladiator!'

'What?' said Specky. 'Are they . . . ?'

'Yep, back together again,' finished Gobba.

'What can I say, Speck?' Danny grinned, shoving his phone back into his pocket. 'Love is complicated. You can't live with 'em, and you can't live without 'em.'

'Obviously!' Specky said. 'Well, good on ya! And, Gob, I almost forgot. I heard you blitzed them in the commentary box today. That's awesome that your voice held up.'

A big smile came across Gobba's face. 'It was

an honour to call you, mate. I can't wait for the day when I'm commentating and you're playing an AFL game. My voice didn't just hold up,' he added, reaching behind his back and pulling a trophy from underneath his jumper. 'It won me this! I won, Speck! I won!'

'Unreal! Nice one, mate!' Specky said, as he took a closer look at the silver-plated cork propped on an engraved base. 'I knew you would! Actually, I've got some news as well.'

Specky told his friends about his All-Australian selection.

'No way! That's awesome!'

'Yep, I made it. I'm off to Ireland.'

Everyone started whooping and yelling all at once, jumping on each other until they all fell to the ground.

'Um, this is so gross!' said Alice, appearing at the front door. 'Once you boys have finished your love-fest, Mum says that my brother has to come and eat something.'

Specky said goodbye to his friends and turned to go back inside. As he closed the door, his mobile vibrated. He pulled it out of his pocket and read the new text message:

You were amazing today! I'm so proud of u. TG xox

PS What were u going to ask me?

Specky sighed. A wave of emotion washed over him as he quickly texted back:

Will u go out with me sometime?

Within seconds another message from Tiger Girl came flying back.

I thought you'd never ask! ☺ *YES! xxx*

DING! DONG!

More visitors? thought Specky, turning back to open the front door.

Specky couldn't believe who was standing there. It was Christina. And behind her he could see her parents in their car, waiting on the street.

'Hi, Speck,' she said, smiling. 'Surprise!'

'Wha . . . what . . . What are you doing here? In Melbourne?' Specky stuttered.

'We were here for the Grand Final. Dad worked on the telecast. You were fantastic!'

'Um, thanks – you should have told me you'd be in town. Are you here for long?'

'Not really, but I convinced my dad to stop by 'cause I wanted to tell you some news. We're moving back to Melbourne, Speck! Well, not until Christmas. I know it feels as if we just moved to Sydney, but my dad's been offered a better job back here. And, well, to be honest . . . I'm really happy I'll be back with my old friends again.'

Specky didn't know what to think or say. He stared at Christina blankly.

'Are you okay?' she asked.

'Um, yeah,' said Specky. 'It's been a long day . . .'

'I know – you must be exhausted. I better get going then. I just wanted to say hi. I can't wait to catch up with you sometime,' she added. 'By the way, as we pulled up we saw this guy drop a parcel here.'

Specky looked down to see a package by his feet. Opening it, he found a box full of Hangar McPhearson books. The note placed on top read: *All first editions and signed by the authors. Congrats, champ! Brad Dobson.*

Specky had to admit, it was a pretty good gift.

'Wow. Is that the entire series? Who sent you those?' asked Christina.

'Just some guy who doesn't get it. Or me.'

'Well, I've got to go,' said Christina, leaning in and giving Specky a kiss on the cheek. 'It's good to see you again, Speck.'

'Yeah, good to see you, too.'

Specky stepped back inside, his stomach now in his throat. He had barely closed the door, when he was startled by a loud knock. It must be Christina again, he thought. What can I say? What if she wants to talk about our relationship?

Specky opened the door, but it wasn't Christina. It was the bald man . . .

23. worldwide

'Simon, my name is George Vernon,' said the man, reaching out to shake Specky's hand. 'I know we have bumped into each other on occasion and you noticed me at your training session at the Punt Road pitch. I'm sorry I wasn't able to stop and explain myself.'

Specky stood there, eyeing him suspiciously. He was immaculately dressed and spoke with a strong English accent.

'Pitch?' said Specky. 'You mean oval? Are you a sports agent? Because I think it's best if you call my parents or talk to my coach. I've already had one guy talk to me about representation and we're not really interested.'

'I'm not a local sports agent, but I guess you

228

could say I'm in the same sort of field,' said the man. 'I'm a worldwide talent scout, and I would certainly like to make a time to talk to your parents.'

'Worldwide?' said Specky. 'For what?'

'Why, for football, of course,' he answered.

'There are no worldwide talent scouts for Aussie Rules.'

'Oh, again, I apologise. I mean soccer. I'm a worldwide talent scout for soccer.'

'Soccer?' repeated Specky. 'What's that got to do with me?'

'Well, the team I represent have talent iden- tifiers all over the world, covering every sport imaginable. You have been on our radar for some eighteen months. Your brilliant athletic ability and your truly spectacular catching talent have convinced us that you're one of six young lads that we are prepared to offer a trial contract to. If you do well, you'd have a shot at becoming a professional footballer with the most famous club in the world.'

Specky was totally confused.

'Um, Mr . . .'

'Vernon.'

'Yeah, Mr Vernon, what exactly are you saying?' asked Specky.

'What I'm saying, young Simon, is that the Manchester United Football Club would like you to come over to the UK and trial with our academy squad as a "soccer" goalie. I'm convinced you have what it takes to make it all the way.'

Specky's jaw dropped. Not in a million years had he seen this coming.

Also available

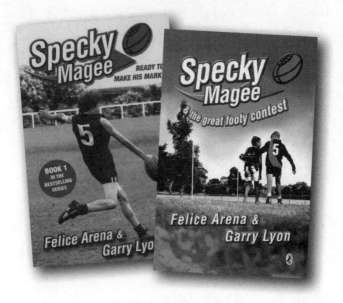

Specky Magee

Simon Magee is twelve and mad about Aussie Rules. He's even got a nickname – 'Specky' – because he takes such spectacular marks, but his family hates footy . . . So why is there a baby photo of him dressed in footy gear? Determined to find out the truth, Specky uncovers more then he ever bargained for. Available from HarperCollins Publishers Australia.

Specky Magee and the Great Footy Contest

Specky comes face to face with a tough, talented player by the name of Derek 'Screamer' Johnson and the two boys become bitter rivals on the field and off. But why is Screamer such a bully? And when a popular TV show runs a nationwide football contest, is Specky good enough to win?

Specky Magee and the Season of Champions

The Lions are playing well and Specky's form is looking good – perhaps good enough to win a scholarship to a prestigious sporting school. But when a knee injury sees him sidelined, Specky soon discovers that there's more to being a champion than just being a legend on the field . . .

Specky Magee and the Boots of Glory

Specky finds himself torn between his old friends and some new team-mates. And his loyalty will be tested – on the field and off – because when he crosses the white line, Booyong becomes his enemy . . . But will his need to solve a school mystery put his footy future in jeopardy?

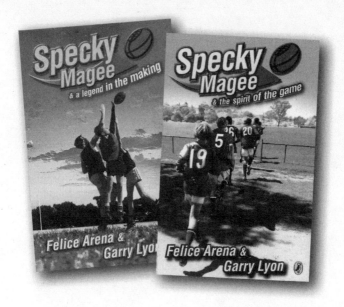

Specky Magee and a Legend in the Making

Specky is once again playing for the Booyong Lions, but things are not the same as when he left. His mates aren't talking to him, no one seems to want him on the team and Screamer seems to be the hero of the day. But Screamer has a secret and Specky is determined to find out what it is . . .

Specky Magee and the Spirit of the Game

Specky can't wait to get to the country and have the chance to play grassroots football for the first time . . . against adults. But more is at stake than the outcome of just one game. Who is Razorback Jack, the mysterious footy hero that Specky keeps hearing about? And what are the boys back at Booyong High up to?

Specky Magee Back to Back #1

Two great Specky books in one! The second and third novels in the series together for the first time in a new collectable edition.